First published in Great Britain in 2008 by Comma Press
www.commapress.co.uk

Versions of 'Claire with Fair Hair,' 'Permanent Granite Sunrise' and 'All Aboard
the Liver Building' were broadcast on Radio 4 (3rd-7th March 08), produced by
Duncan Minshull. 'Mackintosh Willy' was first published in *Alone With Horrors*
(Headline, 1994), 'The Forbidden' was first published in *In the Flesh* (Poseidon,
1986). 'Wide-Eyed' was inspired by the elders in Halewood, Liverpool through
their stories and contributions to the Childhood and Working Lives Project. The
Book of the City series (of which this is the second instalment) is built on four
preceeding pamphlet series, including *Liverpool Stories*, edited by Tane Page.

ISBN 1 905583095
ISBN-13 978 1905583096

The publisher gratefully acknowledges assistance from the Arts Council England
North West, and also the support of Literature Northwest.

Set in Bembo 11/13 by XL Publishing Services, Tiverton
Printed and bound in England by SRP Ltd, Exeter

THE BOOK
OF LIVERPOOL

Edited by
Maria Crossan & Eleanor Rees

Contents

Introduction   vii
ELEANOR REES

Claire with Fair Hair   1
BERYL BAINBRIDGE

Wide-Eyed   7
TRACY ASTON

The Flying Baby of Wavertree   15
BRIAN PATTEN

Permanent Granite Sunrise   19
FRANK COTTRELL BOYCE

Mackintosh Willy   25
RAMSEY CAMPBELL

The Forbidden   43
CLIVE BARKER

Low Visibility   95
MARGARET MURPHY

Something You Don't Have to Deserve   103
JAMES FRIEL

A Different Sky   123
DINESH ALLIRAJAH

CONTENTS

All Aboard the Liver Building   137
PAUL FARLEY

Contributors   145

Introduction

Liverpool is a city submerged in stories: myths rattle in its ears, on the sea breeze, in the seagulls' calls. It's hard to get to the truth of a place like this. Somewhere that shifts and slides, seemingly uncertain of its past and mythologizing its present; an identity both fixed and in flux. Perhaps it's something to do with being on the edge of the land, always looking out to sea? Many of the city's houses seem to face west, as if waiting for something new to emerge over the horizon; a solution, ship or new song?

The range of stories in this anthology reflects the changes undergone by the city over the last six decades or so. The conceit behind the series is to collect stories set over the second half of the last century, from the second world war to the present day and let this ever-present back-drop of historical events emerge on its own terms – the post-war redevelopment of the city, the boom and slump of the 60s and 70s, to the riots in the 80s, the aftermath of the Hillsborough tragedy, right through to the Capital of Culture year.

Liverpool emerges in this anthology as a city still haunted by old ghosts; the past is constantly present. In Beryl Bainbridge's story 'Claire with Fair Hair' it's poetry that provides the spectral link between past and present: an uncanny, disturbing echo. This too is a theme in Brian Patten's story, where the quiet death of a shared memory, a neighbourhood legend, suggests how other city tragedies might also be forgotten, as if taken away on the tide.

How places hold on to memory as a focus for our fears

are key themes in the stories by Ramsey Campbell and Clive Barker. Campbell's story focuses on Newsham Park and a young boy's first encounter with death. Barker also, in his early story 'The Forbidden' finds horrors lurking under the surface of close communities in one of the city's outlying estates. This tale formed the basis for the later blockbusting film franchise *Candyman*; and for all the differences between the two works (the former is set in Liverpool, the latter Chicago) both ring with menacing irony. 'Sweets to the sweet' is one refrain of the story, another in the film: 'I'm the whisper in the playground, the writing on the wall'. Indeed this latter phrase became the name of Liverpool's literature festival. 'The Forbidden' is a story – like many others here – about the ethics of story telling, about what we collectively choose to forget and how we can't help but remember: unconscious histories recurring in the waking dreams of story and art. Liverpool is a city built on suppressed memory bubbling up: the horrors of the slave trade, on sugar and sweetness for some, suffering for others, and this suppression can be seen in the writing that continues to emerge, for instance in its love of the gothic and the ghost story.

Barker's story is set in a close-knit working class community, and exactly what constitutes a sense of belonging and 'at-homeness' is interrogated throughout the anthology. The mass re-housing projects of the late 50s and early 60s, in Tracy Aston's 'Wide-Eyed', provide occasion for optimism, warmth and social cohesion – sentiments that have long since gone sour by the time of Barker's story. Then again, in Dinesh Allirajah's 'A Different Sky' the latest wave of architectural change is registered as the city becomes invaded by luxury apartments and new investment. Again we find optimism tinged with loss, a sense that with change and progress something else may well be forgotten. Maybe this is why Liverpool is so hard to capture in words: it changes constantly, socially and economically. It has a rise and fall just like the Mersey.

INTRODUCTION

The periods of deprivation and turmoil are undeniable. The early 80s are seen through Margaret Murphy's story, set on the fringe of the Toxteth riots, a story of personal empowerment that puts the individual at the heart of the cultural moment. In Jim Friel's tale of an ordinary Sunday night at the local club, it's the spectre of Hillsborough that pervades. Elsewhere, people's stories stand as resolutely as the buildings themselves. Frank Cottrell Boyce's 'Permanent Granite Sunrise' tells a very personal story about one man's sense of purpose through the well-documented history of the city's two cathedrals. This is a story about how people find continuity and a sense of identity in relation to things external to themselves, to buildings and other people, and how we use them to protect us from the passing of time, from loss.

In the final story, Paul Farley teases the fierce Liverpudlian sense of home and identity and asks us to look to beyond this, to the future, not as something haunted or still resounding with trauma, but unclaimed, unknown. Through the metaphor of the sea, he implores us to look outwards, to 'move on'. Change does seem to be key to the Liverpool experience. I have a sense, made all the stronger by these stories, that we are all involved in a process of dreaming, telling and writing a city into being, always with an eye on the horizon – for a change in the weather or a storm coming in from the west – trying collectively to keep the city anchored to the shore.

Eleanor Rees
May 2008

Claire with Fair Hair

Beryl Bainbridge

That first Saturday in 1949 Mrs Hemans accompanied George into town on foot although they could have caught the tram on Wavertree Road. She said it was too risky mingling with the street urchins who rode without paying and whose legs were spotty with vermin bites; she didn't want him scratching when he met Mrs Ackerly.

They plodded down Brownlow Hill, turned left opposite the Adelphi Hotel, walked on past Central Station and reached the Lyceum Tea Rooms at the bottom end of Bold Street. Here Mrs Hemans stopped for a moment to point out the ruins of a church which had been bombed in the May Blitz and where she said her father had once sung in the choir of a Sunday. Grandad died during the war on account of his rushing about being a Home Guard. Mother said his death was caused by the strain of carrying heavy buckets of water to douse out fires. Father said he knew for a fact that Grandad's passing on had been due to his tripping over the kerbstone outside a pub in Paradise Street.

'Now listen,' said Mother, 'you're to pay attention to whatever Mrs Ackerly tells you to do. It's for your future.'

When George was nine – he was now ten – Mrs Hemans had decided she wanted her son to have a job as a bank clerk. She had been a cleaner in the Westminster Bank in Wavertree for some years and it seemed to her to be a respectable profession and one with short hours. The dilemma was that all the men behind the grilles spoke very proper, like people on the wireless, and she was well aware that George's

1

speech was somewhat lacking in this respect. Then, quite by chance, she had come across an advertisement in the *Liverpool Echo* for elocution lessons given by a lady on the top floor of Crane Hall, the piano factory. Having saved up enough money, today was to be the beginning of George's future life.

Crane Hall was a five storey building on Hanover Street, a thoroughfare leading down to the River Mersey and the Salthouse Dock. There was a side door and a porter smoking a pipe in a cubicle. He asked them what they wanted and Mother told him they had come to see Mrs Ackerly. He said, 'It's on the fourth floor,' and Mother retorted, 'I know that. I have an appointment.'

The ground floor room was stocked with pianos shiny as sunlight. At one, an old man crouched on a stool, head to one side, middle finger stabbing at the same key, over and over. A black dog sat beside him, one paw raised.

'He's a piano tuner,' explained Mother, pushing George into the lift. 'They're all blind.' He knew she wasn't referring to the dog.

Mrs Ackerly had a mouth painted bright red and used a cigarette holder when she smoked. She was wearing trousers and a frilly blouse. Her cigarette lighter was shaped like a bullet and made of gold.

'This is George,' Mother said, nudging him into a smile.

Mother stayed for that first lesson, which was all about breathing in and out, and humming. Mrs Ackerly stood behind him, holding his shoulders back. He got the giggles, which made Mother frown, but Mrs Ackerly said that often she too found it funny, and patted his shoulder.

Going down in the lift they were accompanied by a young girl with yellow hair who smiled at him, sweetly. He smiled back and Mother said, 'There's nothing to smile about… I just hope I'm not throwing away good money.'

The next Saturday he went on his own to Crane Hall. The old man was there again, at a different piano, his dog in attendance, paw held aloft. For a moment, crossing towards

2

the lift gates, George thought the dog was waving at him.

Mrs Ackerly said that an ability to pronounce words properly had mainly to do with control of the lung, an apparatus, acting like bellows, that enabled one to be fluent.

'Repeat after me,' she said, puffing out smoke, 'Claire has fair hair.'

'Cler has fer her,' he copied.

'No,' she said, 'you are not using your apparatus.'

Most Saturdays the young girl joined him in the lift. She said she worked on the second floor which surprised him because he thought they were about the same age and that neither of them was old enough to have a job. He wanted to ask what her name was but lacked the courage.

Slowly, he became interested in the business of talking proper. Mrs Ackerly said that some of his wrong pronunciation of words was not entirely due to his breathing: it had quite a bit to do with the Irish arriving in Liverpool, along with the Jews and the Chinese. 'They've distorted the language,' she said.

When George told Mother this, Father got angry. He said it was outrageous of Mrs Ackerly to cast aspersions on the Irish. But then, as Mother ranted, who minded what she cast just as long as their son ended up getting a posh job when he was older.

A month later the girl in the lift asked George if he wanted to see where she worked. She said that when his lesson was over he was to get out on the second floor and she'd be waiting for him.

Mrs Ackerly was urging him to think up sentences of his own that would help his speech. When he recited, 'How now, brown cow,' she said that was something she'd already told him; he must think of something fresh. He blurted out, 'Bloody Bootle boys get bitten by bloody bed bugs,' at which she commented that it was a good try but that she hadn't been thinking of alliteration. Then she gave him a poem to read which began –

3

> The boy stood on the burning deck
> Whence all but he had fled;
> The flame that lit the battle's wreck
> Shone round him o'er the dead.

'It's all about days gone by,' she told him, 'though you should realise that the past is ever present.'

Before he left she said he was coming on very well and bade him learn the poem off by heart. She'd chosen it because it had been composed by a Liverpool woman called Felicia Hemans. It was interesting wasn't it, she queried that they shared the same name?

When he got out of the lift on the second floor, the girl wasn't there. He was in a corridor lit by gas lamp. He thought he heard singing, and the twanging of a piano. After some minutes he tiptoed along the corridor, turned a corner and came to a door marked Front Stalls. He was standing there, hesitating, when the door burst open and the girl appeared. She had one finger raised to her mouth, bidding him to keep quiet. Behind her the singing was very loud, like the wireless on full blast when Father listened to Henry Hall's Guest Night. She beckoned him down steps into a large space filled with dim rows of empty seats. There was a man in front waving his arms about. The girl led him, stumbling, through darkness; finally hissed at him to sit down. When he looked up, his mouth opened in wonderment.

Before him, lit by footlights, he saw a raised platform with the front half of an ancient ship jutting outwards, its sails hanging loose, and behind, a backcloth painted with flames leaping wildly upwards. Three men in old fashioned uniforms were standing on the deck of the ship, clutching their throats and writhing as though in pain. The singing got louder but there was so much screaming and firing of guns that he couldn't make out the words.

'It's the Battle of the Nile,' the girl whispered, 'but you know that, don't you?'

He didn't tell Mother what he'd seen because she didn't seem to think he was late home, even though he knew he'd been away for hours. And when he mentioned he'd made friends with the girl who had been in the lift that first Saturday, she shouted, 'Don't talk balderdash. There was only me and you.' He would have liked to ask where and what the Nile was but Father was too busy reading the paper.

He couldn't wait for the next Saturday to come, nor for the lesson to be over. The girl wasn't waiting for him outside the lift but he knew she'd expect him to come through that door at the end of the corridor. She was standing above him, peering down over the glow of the footlights, waving at him to join her. He didn't know how to get there until a man below her rose up out of the darkness and pointed a white stick to the right of the stage; it was the piano tuner. 'Claire,' he shouted, 'tell him what we want.'

It wasn't that difficult, the thing he was asked to do, which was to stand on that half of a ship and speak his poem. He did it rather well, he thought, but the blind man made him repeat it. In the middle of his second uttering of the lines –

'Speak Father, once again he cried,

If I may yet be gone,

And but the booming shots replied,

And fast the flames rolled on' – so much smoke billowed up around him that he couldn't stop coughing.

'Good, good,' shouted the blind man.

Then a stout man in a scarlet jacket and white stockings shook George's hand and wished him good luck. 'I appreciate what you did,' he said, voice husky. 'You're a son to be proud of.'

The following Saturday George was again asked to recite his poem. This time, standing there, he no longer felt shy. He could feel the rocking of the ship, smell the gunpowder, sense that something exciting was about to happen.

There came a burst of thunder sound

The boy, oh where was he?
Ask of the winds that far around
With fragments strewed the sea.

When it came to the end of the last two lines, which stressed that the noblest thing that had perished was a young and faithful heart, there was a tumultuous outbreak of clapping and voices shouting out 'Bravo'. Peer as he did, he couldn't make out anyone occupying the seats below. The girl was in her usual position, sitting in a corner, weeping, a shawl covering her fair hair.

When George didn't return that afternoon Mrs Hemans hurried down to question Mrs Ackerly, who said she'd last seen him at eleven o' clock that morning. The blind man, for obvious reasons, was of little help. That evening Mother informed the police and a search of the building was made, including the locked second and third floors and the several small dressing rooms at the back of the stage. George's school cap was hanging on a peg. Nobody could work out how it had got there because that part of the building had been locked up for years and there were no footprints on the dusty floors. Although there was no trace of a fire, a mysterious and powerful smell of charred wood hung in the air.

Mrs Ackerly told Mrs Hemans that Crane Hall had started out as a piano depository in 1911, but two years later the middle section had been converted to the Neptune Theatre. Intermittently, in the 20s and 30s it had been used in this way, but the war had put a stop to it.

George never came home. Mrs Ackerly sent a copy of the verses he'd been learning to his mother, hoping it would bring comfort. It didn't, particularly the bit about the flames rolling on and the boy not budging.

Mr Hemans took the poem into the back yard, and having read it, tears springing in his eyes, squashed the bit of paper in his fist. There were too many references to a brave young lad standing his ground until his dad appeared.

6

Wide-Eyed

Tracy Aston

My great gran is planning something. I can tell, coz she's got this look in her eye, like she's gone somewhere in her head. And when she gets that look, you can bet that something is going to happen. Mam and dad don't seem to notice it, but I know. And if I say, 'What are you up to Gran?' She just says, 'Wait and see child. Wait and see.' When they said we had to move out of our house coz they were going to knock the whole street down, she got that look then. Well, she got really angry first, I mean, *scary* angry. Not like when me and our Billy, that's my brother Billy, not my dad Billy, decided we were going to run away to sea and hid in the docks waiting for a chance to sneak on board our dad's ship then got brought home by a policeman. Or like when we dressed our Jean up in her pram and did penny for the guy. She was angry then, but she didn't shout. She doesn't have to shout, just looks at you, my gran, and you know. But this time she was shouting. Things like, 'Over my dead body!' and 'Bloody Corpy!' She didn't swear either, but she swore then, for days.

And then she got her old photos out and showed me all the people who grew up in our house. There were loads! And that wasn't even all of them, coz they didn't have money for photos much in the old days. And then she got that look in her eye. Bedlam, Mam called it. First Gran started a petition. And that got her swearing again coz not everyone would sign it. 'Bloody indoor toilets!' she said. 'That's what it is. And what's wrong, I'd like to know, with

7

a lavvy in the yard?' I didn't tell her I liked the idea of an indoor toilet coz I was scared of the dark, and spiders. 'And if they can't cope with the yard, what's wrong with a guzzunder?' But Mam wouldn't let us use a potty of a night. She thought that was common. But Gran was rowing in the street over it, and swearing I reckon. But Mam wouldn't let me out so I couldn't tell for sure. All the old people signed. But it did no good though. Then she got me to help her make posters, coz her writing's a bit wobbly now, with 'SAVE OUR STREET' and 'DOWN WITH THE CORPY' in red crayon. The old people put them in their windows. But that did no good either. Then just as we're loading the last of our stuff into the removal van, Father Gerry comes and persuades Gran to untie herself from our big brass door knob. And then she cried.

I was sad in one way, but excited too. I tried not to let Gran see that, but she knew anyway coz she said, 'You're bound to be excited child. You don't know what you're losing yet.' And I didn't know what she meant. That was February.

Me and Jean have got our own bedroom and Billy's not allowed in it unless he's got sweets. And dad got a special downstairs room built at the back for Gran coz she can't do stairs anymore and had to sleep in the parlour in our old house. It's just big enough for a bed, a little table, a wardrobe and her piano. And we've got a garden front and back, but they still haven't put grass on it. And we've got gas, but they didn't switch it on for a bit so we had chippy dinners. That was good. And they haven't put shops up so Mam shops mostly at the moby at the end of the road. They've got everything in that van! Everything we want anyway. We were one of the first to move in, but now all the houses are full. But we don't see the people much. Mam says they're probably still settling in. As soon as we moved, Gran kept saying, 'This street's too wide.' I say, 'Too wide for what Gran?' But all she'll say is, 'You'll see.' And that's when she started getting that look in her eye.

Me and Mam are going to town one day and she says, 'Let's go and see what they've done with our street.' But when we turn the corner, she stops, and so do I. It looks like those pictures from the war, when there's just rubble. Then we walk to where our house used to be. It made me feel funny. A bit like when I left my doll on the ferry after me and Mam had been to see Auntie Kathleen who's gone all posh coz she moved over the water. I found a bit of wall from our bedroom where Billy had scrawled 'Liverpool F C Rules' with his crayons. He got a belt for that. But I kept the bit of wall. I look at Mam. She's got tears in her eyes. Then she says, 'Best not tell your gran.'

When we get back, Gran's got a man in tuning her piano. That makes me feel better coz she hasn't played it since we got told about moving. I know she can't play when she's sad so I think this means she's settling in. When Mam's mam died, that's Gran's daughter, Mam said she didn't play for six months. Gran's lived longer than all her children and Mam says the way Gran's going, she'll be playing at *her* funeral, but I try not to think about things like that. Gran's piano is *really really* old. Even older than Gran. Her mam got it from this Jewish family she did cleaning for. They were getting a new one so they let her have it. Gran said they had to bring it on a cart coz there were no removal vans in the old days, then they had to take the parlour window out to get it in the house!

Gran says she's out of practice so she's been playing every day. But I still don't know what she's up to. We've been playing in the street when the weather's nice, but no-one else has come out. And we know there are children in number three, number ten, and number fourteen coz we've seen them coming in and out. 'I told you,' said Gran, 'The street's too wide. Makes people keep themselves to themselves. And to put the tin hat on it, they've given people gardens. And there's no steps in front to sit out on.' I ask Gran if the other people in the street might be from a different country, where maybe they're not used to mixing in. And *maybe* there's something we could do to show people how to mix. 'Great minds,' says Gran. 'Great minds.' And she goes off to do some more practising.

But now it's summer, I think everyone will play out. Even the mams and dads come out of an evening. But since our dad left going to sea he's been working on the docks, and by the time he gets the bus home it's nearly our bedtime so he's going to miss out. Summer's the best apart from Christmas and it lasts for *a-g-e-s*! The new tarmac's soft and bubbly with the sun and we're playing with it when Gran goes up the street to use the phone. Then our Jean says, 'Why don't we go and knock for someone?' So we go to number three. They've got a boy and a girl, about as big as our Billy. The lady comes to the door and when I ask if they want to come out to play, she says, 'They're playing in the garden at the moment.' But she never asked us in so we went back in the street. That's another thing, no-one comes in our house and we don't go in theirs. Mam used to say our old house was like Piccadilly Circus. But I think she liked that. We never hear anyone going, 'It's only me,' and then just walking in anymore.

Me and Jean and Billy have been playing out for three days in a row now and *still* no-one else has come out. After tea Gran told us to get washed and put clean clothes on but she won't say why. Mam's asked her what's going on but she just says, 'Wait and see,' with, by the way, that look in her eye. It's half past six and Gran's on pins, pacing about and looking out the window, and humming. The she'll have a bit of a sing, then she's at the front door looking up the street. Then at seven, she claps her hands and says, 'They're here!' Then up the street comes dad, and two old men, an old lady and a man about dad's age. They're all carrying things. Dad's got bags, and the three old ones have got black cases.

They get to the door and make a big fuss of Gran, then Mam, then me and Jean and Billy all get our hair ruffled. It turns out it's mam's Uncle Frank, dad's Uncle Bill and Auntie Nelly and Mam's cousin Charlie. Dad's brought beer and pop and they've brought a squeeze box, a guitar, a fiddle and a mouth organ. We're going to have a party! Mam says, 'Tea first,' and puts the kettle on. I'm thinking they're going in the front room and so does Mam, but then they start talking about the best way to get Gran's piano in the street! Mam's not happy. 'What will the neighbours say?' 'Hopefully, they'll be too busy singing to say anything,' says Gran. 'This isn't like our old street,' says Mam. 'You don't need to tell me,' says Gran. 'And that's the point.' Mam says she's keeping out of it. She doesn't want any trouble and the neighbours barely say hello as it is. 'Then we've nothing to lose,' says Gran. Dad and Charlie heave the piano through the door and up the path while I keep Jean and Billy out the way. Then Dad sets a table up on the pavement and puts the beer and pop on it. I get the glasses, coz Mam's got a face on in the kitchen.

When I take the glasses out I can see net curtains twitching across the road. And as they're settling down with their instruments they're talking about how Gran got the priest dancing on Coronation Day and how they used to do this *every Friday* when the weather was good and how they couldn't remember why they got out of the habit. Then they start. It's a 'Long Way to Tipperary' gets number fourteen, number sixteen and number eleven out. None of them look very happy though. 'We'll Meet Again' gets number fifteen out. She's one of the smallest ladies I've ever seen and looks almost as old as Gran. She watches for a minute then marches towards us. She's nearly reached us when I can hear her singing. She carries on as she shakes hands with everyone.

11

Then the children from number fourteen run over. Then me and Jean and Billy hold hands in a circle and dance. Not proper dancing, more like ring-a-ring-a-roses.

By the time they've finished 'When the Red Red Robin Comes Bob Bob Bobbing Along' *most* of the neighbours have come over, even the ones that looked cross. Only number five isn't there. Then Gran starts 'The White Cliffs of Dover' and everyone's singing and *Mam* comes out and smiles at Dad. I grab our Billy and we start waltzing the way Gran taught me and everyone claps us at the end. Then dad puts his arms round Mam and starts singing 'Let Me Call You Sweetheart' and Gran gets a tear in her eye.

I knew she would coz she told me that Great Grandad used to sing that to her when they were courting. *Then* the *grown-ups* start dancing! Then they have a break and dad passes glasses of beer round and everyone's talking. But they stop for a minute when they see a police car pull up outside number five. Mam looks at dad. Dad says, 'Let's just see what they say.' And then, what seems like ages later, the policeman brings Mister number five out in a wheel chair and they're coming up the street. Mister number five is called Jack Gladwin, and it turns out that the policeman, Sergeant Murphy, is his son-in-law. *And* Jack Gladwin's got a telephone! And coz Jack's daughter is in hospital having a baby, Jack rang the sergeant coz he wanted to join in the party! Sergeant Murphy says we can carry on but not too late and as long as we don't get any complaints. Jack Gladwin has brought a pair of spoons! And when 'Pack Up Your Troubles in Your Old Kit Bag' starts, he bashes the spoons on his hand and his legs really fast, even though he's very old. Everyone claps at the end and Mam gives him a glass of beer, then him and Gran and the tiny lady get chatting, I think about the old days probably.

At half past ten everyone is still singing and dancing, except our Jean who fell asleep on Mam's knee and got taken to bed, and people from the next street have joined in! Then at eleven, dad says they'd better think about stopping but it would be good to do it again, and everyone claps and cheers. Then dad sings 'I'll Take You Home Again Kathleen' and everyone dances. And Gran looks really happy. I hear Jack Gladwin say, 'She's a real character.' Uncle Frank says, 'She's a character all right.' Dad says he could think of other ways to describe her and they all laugh, but he didn't say what ways.

The next day I ask Gran if she'll teach me how to play the piano. 'I thought you'd never ask,' she says. 'It's good to pass things on.' I show Gran my bit of wall with 'Liverpool F C Rules' on it. She nods and smiles then goes and gets her box of photos and gives it to me. She says, 'Look after the memories child. In the end, they're all we have.'

The Flying Baby of Wavertree

Brian Patten

Eddie stood on the demolition site staring at what little remained of the street in which he'd grown up. It had been a narrow little street full of narrow little houses, all of which would have looked the same had people not painted their doors different colours. The front parlours all opened out onto the pavement. There were no corridors or vestibules – you opened the door and there was the world, waiting for you with its rotting teeth and bad breath and nosy-parker eyes. There had been no trees in the street, just a couple of privet hedges and wild lilac bushes that grew on a patch of wasteland where the house he'd been born in had been. The house had been destroyed during the Second World War, and the bombsite where it had stood had become known as the Flying Baby's Garden. His garden.

Eddie had no memory of the incident, but it seems he had been blown out of the upstairs bedroom window, and had landed in the street, miraculously unharmed and still asleep on the mattress from his cot. His was one of the neighbourhood's few good luck stories – if you can call having your home bombed and being blown out the window good luck.

Though the story had entered local mythology, Eddie had never volunteered the fact that the baby had been himself. Though he nearly had once. That was when he'd been a child, playing on the bombsite with his friends. But the words had stuck in his throat, and he'd panicked and fought for breath. For some years afterwards he'd felt anxious

15

at even the possibility of the story being brought up. Then in his teens he'd convinced himself he was disinterested in it.

In Eddie's earliest memories the street had been cobbled and lit by gas lamps to which he and his friends tied ropes, which they used as swings. Even the houses had been lit by gaslight when he was very young. Gas mantles produced a different kind of light from electricity. The shadows cast by human beings seem insubstantial now, he thought, but they were once something special: those created by gaslight were thick and black and as rich as tar. He remembered how, when he walked along the street between the lamps, his shadow was constantly growing then shrinking then growing again. And how if it was a windy night the street lamps would splutter and his shadow would wobble about as if it were drunk, or trying to escape and go off to lead a life of its own. Electric light stole the souls from shadows. It flattened them out and robbed them of characteristics they had possessed since humankind had invented fire and made their doppelgängers dance.

After the bombing raid his grandparents had taken him in. The house had always seemed dark to Eddie. It was a darkness that had nothing to do with the lack of sunlight. It was more to do with the misfortune that had befallen them.

The hub of the house was the kitchen, which was constantly damp due to a dripping clotheshorse that hung from the ceiling. Then there was a small front parlour, a bedroom and a box room big enough for a single bed. That was it. There was no bathroom and the toilet – which froze up in winter – was outside in the yard.

His gran had been born in 1898. As a girl she had worked as a dancer in local variety theatre. She told him she'd been happy then. There was a photograph of her somewhere, wearing a fox-fur and a gigantic hat. In the photograph she was smiling. Later she and his grandfather had been publicans for a while, running one of the big locals. But then the

Second World War came, and everything changed.

During the first week of May 1941 Liverpool experienced its heaviest bombing raids of the whole war. In those few nights around 650 planes dropped 900 tonnes of high explosives and over a hundred thousand firebombs on the city, killing over 1,700 people. The newsreels never showed images of Liverpool burning. The true extent of the raids went unreported for fear of lowering the country's morale. All the country knew was that there had been a number of 'incidents' in a northern city. In Anfield a thousand people were buried in a mass grave. Eddie's mother had been amongst them.

The story of the Flying Baby was one he was to hear again and again – the miraculous child lifted whole and unscathed from the burning debris, while the city's morgues spilled over and a huge charnel pit was being dug in Anfield. He'd heard it retold umpteen times. The people telling it and the people listening inevitably shook their heads and smiled at the baby's luck. There was such a thing as good fortune, their faces said. Miracles can happen, even in the most ordinary places, even in the harshest times. Good fortune? Luck? He didn't think so.

By the time he was an adult the story had faded into the background, and in the last dozen or so years he had only come across mention of it once.

Now here he was again, back in the old neighbourhood. He'd returned on a whim after hearing that the area was being demolished. The cavernous Victorian pub his grandparents had once managed was still standing defiantly amongst the rubble, but few other landmarks remained. Inside the pub had been a barman and a solitary drinker, and though they were a good twenty years younger than him, Eddie and the two men were soon swapping stories about the neighbourhood's past. The barman, who'd known nothing of the Anfield grave, recalled how in 1973 the press had reported the discovery of a different mass grave.

It had been a few miles away in Old Swan, where the remains of 3,500 bodies had been unearthed when builders were digging the foundations for a new school. Had the site been the scene of a mass murder? Or had it been a plague pit? The Home Office had ordered that the bodies be cremated, and no final explanation for the grave had been forthcoming. Now a mere five years after the discovery, that story too had receded.

It was Eddie who surprised himself by bringing up the story of the Flying Baby. Maybe the ghosts of his grandparents were watching over him, maybe that was why he'd felt so much at ease, but whatever… It seemed the most natural thing in the world to want to mention it.

But neither of the two men knew the story, which left Eddie feeling confused. It was as if by not knowing about the flying baby they had somehow betrayed him, and themselves, and their past. The conversation drifted, and the story remained untold. He wondered if the bar was to be the place in which his story would finally die, for individual stories did die, he guessed, like people. Either that, or they were subsumed into the greater stories and lost.

Eddie stood on the demolition site and tried to imagine where the house he had been born in had stood, but of course he could not remember. He had been far too young when it had been bombed. And his mother, that sweet woman who had ended up being dropped into a forgotten mass grave – she had also been young.

Permanent Granite Sunrise

Frank Cottrell Boyce

Dedicated to Jim Brady – a true gentleman whose real-life work inspired this work of fiction

The first time Ronald Brady saw the cathedral, it was floating in the air above the playground of St. Sylvester's Primary School.

The playground railings were decorated with tin foil in honour of the visit of Archbishop Downey, who had come to tell them his plans for the new cathedral. A tiny man with a big voice, the Archbishop had set words dancing round the room like flashes of light from a prism – exotic, bewildering words – buttress, cupola, nave, narthex, triumph. The cathedral he described was not the celebrated concrete wigwam you can see today. He was after something altogether more stupendous. A forest of granite columns sheltering fifty-three altars, aisles like rivers, a narthex – a vast space always open, always warm, for the use of the destitute – and all shouldering a dome five hundred and ten feet high. 'Twice the height,' said the Archbishop, 'of the dome of St. Paul's Cathedral in London.' When he said the word London you could hear that it was the location as well as the denomination of Wren's masterpiece that meant that it had to be dwarfed.

He told them how Chartres had been built by common people and by aristocrats working together, singing hymns as they hauled the stones, built of prayers and hope, and most of all, charity. Then he pulled out his tin and asked them for their thrupennces. He gave them each a picture of the waterfront and Liver buildings. 'When you get outside,' he said, 'hold that picture up to the sky, hold it up to God.'

When Ronald did that, he saw for the first time the imaginary cathedral dwarfing the waterfront, rising over the city like a permanent granite sunrise.

By the time Ronald had left school, building work had started, and he went as apprentice to a big Glaswegian – Tony Backland – one of fifty master bricklayers. Ronald carried his hod, fetched his tea, and watched him spreading cement on the bricks like butter, snapping them into place. 'Are you watching this?' he'd ask from time to time. 'Mr. Backland,' said Ronald, 'the rate you go, this thing'll be up before I've served my time.' Watching Tony made his fingers itch.

Sometimes they'd see the Archbishop wandering round the site with the gent with the big moustaches. 'Lutyens,' said Tony, 'Greatest architect in the whole empire. Better than theirs any day.'

Theirs was Gilbert Scott White – designer of the telephone box – who was already at work at the other end of Hope Street, building the rival Anglican cathedral, a gothic, ecclesiastical version of his Battersea Power Station, a wretched three hundred feet high. Two cathedrals being built at the same time on the same street – a giant epistemological derby game played out in bricks and sweat.

'You are building a cathedral for our times,' said Downey – a dig at the phoney medievalism of the Anglican one. 'It will be visible miles out to sea. And it will be consecrated, not to a saint, but to Christ himself.'

Well there were short men with big egos goading each other on all over Europe at the time. Franco, Mussolini, Hitler, Stalin. And when their chips were down, it was big men with no egos who marched away.

Tony Backland was among the first.

He spent his last day showing Ronald every trick and short cut he knew, and handed him his trowel. 'Got the Cardinal to bless that the day he laid the corner stone,' he said. Then he took a last look at the job – they were working on one of the groins at the entrance to the crypt. 'See that you finish this before I get back,' he said.

Ronald was fifteen, too young to sign up. Half a dozen went with Tony. A dozen more a few weeks later. Some of the Irish went back home. There were fewer and fewer people on the site, so that soon the Archbishop came to know Ronald by name and would ask him how it was going and sometimes look high into the air, as if he could see the cupola, the dome, the triumph.

By 1942 they'd all gone but Ronald. He turned up punctually every day, and everyday dispatched fifty hods of bricks all by himself, one lone teenager executing the fantasies of architects and archbishops. The press cottoned on to him and he was for a while a symbol of steadfastness, and hope. From time to time, the archbishop would have his photo taken with him for papers in America, Australia and Russia. The last time, they both looked into the sky together but this time they were looking not for triumph but for bombers. It was May and the Blitz had started. Night after night, bombs fell, filling the city with absences. A smoking space, where the Rotunda once stood. Flowers, where this family had been. Some people sheltered in the newly completed cathedral crypt. Ronald stayed with them – it would be handy for the morning. In the restless hours, he seemed to feel his unbuilt cathedral above his head, frail as a barrage balloon in the burning night.

When he came up the next morning, and the cathedral wasn't there, it took him a moment to remember that this was because he hadn't finished building it. He rolled up his sleeves and set to.

But the truth was it did burn down in those fires. The war left the city with no money and the world with no will for the colossal. The crypt was finished off and roofed in like a stone field. Downey walked across his still subterranean dream, staring balefully at his Anglican rival – two hundred feet in the air.

When he died, the diocese had a rethink and held a competition. Downey had wanted something modern, they said, how about this? Five years later they threw up something that looked like the Apollo command module reworked in concrete and glass. You can't get much more modern than that. Concrete seems the most appropriate material, they said, for this modern age – classless, urban, durable, industrial. You didn't need a pipe-smoking medieval craftsman to put that up.

Ronald went to the opening but never made it into the building. Walking past the crypt entrance, he spotted a bit of mortar that needed retouching. Made a note of it. And was soon lost in compiling a to-do list, his eye drifting upwards, tracing the lines of bricks and columns that were not there. And that was the way of it from then on. A couple of times a week – working on this hospital or that school – he'd find himself laying down the Blessed Trowel of Tony Backland, pushing back his cap and thinking, there's something I'm supposed to do. Then he'd remember that the something was build a cathedral.

Marriage and children made it better for a while but the children who filled your life with noise and duty only gave you bigger, more aching absences when they left. If he started any job, he had to keep going till he finished it. Decorating the living room, he'd work on through the night and into the next day, urgent and incessant as though the Vymura on the trestle table was a patient on the operating table whose heart might give out any minute. He once built an outrigger extension to the kitchen – floor, drains, the lot – in a single sleepless weekend. When it was time to clear the gutters, he'd work his way along the whole terrace, and would have cleared the gutters of the whole city if it had

22

been legal. At night, he'd flop into bed and still have that feeling that something was left undone. Had he locked the back door? Yes. What then? He still hadn't built the bloody cathedral.

He tried to shun the cathedral thinking that would help shake off the unceasing, gnawing feeling, but he was drawn to it. He became a tour guide for a while, showing visitors around the place. Mostly he showed them round the crypt. Standing in its dark arches he could still recover that sense of the finished thing ballooning over his head somewhere. And although he was normally quiet, he'd talk and talk down there, trying to delay the moment that he would have to come up the steps and see that empty space still there – its vastness only emphasised by the presence of that tiny concrete cake tin. He'd walk the visitors round the new cathedral showing them, pointing to the empty air and telling them what would have been there. 'The nave, that would've gone this way – half a mile – up to the high altar – twelve feet above the floor...' In the end the Provost had to have a word. 'They've come to see something that is here, not something that isn't,' he said.

'The thing that isn't,' thought Ronald, 'is the point of my life.'

On duty one morning, a big country-looking fella in a suit greeted him. He had an accent but Ronald wasn't sure what it was. It could've been Norwegian. 'I've not been before,' he said. 'My dad worked here.'

'Was your dad a priest then?'

The big man laughed. 'A bricklayer. Before the war. His name was Tony Backland.'

'I remember Tony. How is he?'

'Dead.'

'Oh, sorry.'

'I didn't know him. He's just a big blank space to me. He went to Normandy and never came back. He was twenty three. My mum moved to Canada. The wide open spaces.

This is my first time here.'

'Twenty three. He seemed like an old man to me.'

'Well that's a thing he never got to be.'

It had never struck him till then that Tony might be dead. That all of them were very likely dead.

'Tony didn't work on this place,' said Ronald. 'He worked downstairs. Come and I'll show you.'

He took him down to the crypt and showed him the walls, the groins, the arches that his dad had built, described the quickness of his hand and the accuracy of his eye. 'He made his mark alright. He made this. And he made you.'

The big man nodded but didn't seem inclined to move. Ronald carried on, describing the cathedral that Tony had had in his mind when he laid those bricks. Columns, cupola, narthex, altars, dome. He never interrupted. Ronald never looked up. He looked into the lad's face and saw that he was seeing it, rising above them on the other side of the ceiling. I'd love to tell you that he took out the little picture Downey had given him but that had perished long ago. He just kept talking and as he talked he had a sense of shedding, of losing something, of finishing something. And suddenly in the big man's eyes he saw the cathedral was there, where it was meant to be – vast and weightless, taking up the space where something else should have been. A cathedral invisible to all the busy, fleshy lives because it was built of air – the appropriate material for anyone and everyone who had lost someone, something, sometime. A cathedral that was rising as he spoke into the empty space left behind by every loss, rising like a permanent sunrise.

Mackintosh Willy

Ramsey Campbell

To start with, he wasn't called Mackintosh Willy. I never knew who gave him that name. Was it one of those nicknames that seem to proceed from a group subconscious, names recognised by every member of the group yet apparently originated by none? One has to call one's fears something, if only to gain the illusion of control. Still, sometimes I wonder how much of his monstrousness we created. Wondering helps me not to ponder my responsibility for what happened at the end.

When I was ten I thought his name was written inside the shelter in the park. I saw it only from a distance; I wasn't one of those who made a game of braving the shelter. At ten I wasn't afraid to be timid – that came later, with adolescence.

Yet if you had walked past Newsham Park you might have wondered what there was to fear: why were children advancing, bold but wary, on the red-brick shelter by the twilit pool? Surely there could be no danger in the shallow shed, which might have held a couple of dozen bicycles. By now the fishermen and the model boats would have left the pool alone and still; lamps on the park road would have begun to dangle luminous tails in the water. The only sounds would be the whispering of children, the murmur of trees around the pool, perhaps a savage incomprehensible muttering whose source you would be unable to locate. Only a game, you might reassure yourself.

And of course it was: a game to conquer fear. If you had

waited long enough you might have heard shapeless movement in the shelter, and a snarling. You might have glimpsed him as he came scuttling lopsidedly out of the shelter, like an injured spider from its lair. In the gathering darkness, how much of your glimpse would you believe? The unnerving swiftness of the obese limping shape? The head that seemed to belong to another, far smaller, body, and was almost invisible within a grey Balaclava cap, except for the small eyes which glared through the loose hole?

All of that made us hate him. We were too young for tolerance – and besides, he was intolerant of us. Ever since we could remember he had been there, guarding his territory and his bottle of red biddy. If anyone ventured too close he would start muttering. Sometimes you could hear some of the words: 'Damn bastard prying interfering snooper... thieving bastard layabout... think you're clever, eh?... I'll give you something clever...'

We never saw him until it was growing dark: that was what made him into a monster. Perhaps during the day he joined his cronies elsewhere – on the steps of ruined churches in the centre of Liverpool, or lying on the grass in St John's Gardens, or crowding the benches opposite Edge Hill Public Library, whose stopped clock no doubt helped their draining of time. But if anything of this occurred to us, we dismissed it as irrelevant. He was a creature of the dark.

Shouldn't this have meant that the first time I saw him in daylight was the end? In fact, it was only the beginning.

It was a blazing day at the height of summer, my tenth. It was too hot to think of games to while away my school holidays. All I could do was walk errands for my parents, grumbling a little.

They owned a small newsagent's on West Derby Road. That day they were expecting promised copies of the *Tuebrook Bugle*. Even when he disagreed with them, my father always supported the independent papers – the *Bugle*, the *Liverpool Free Press*: at least they hadn't been swallowed or destroyed by a monopoly. The lateness of the *Bugle* worried him; had the paper given in? He sent me to find out.

I ran across West Derby Road just as the traffic lights at the top of the hill released a flood of cars. Only girls used the pedestrian subway so far as I was concerned; besides, it was flooded again. I strolled past the concrete police station into the park, to take the long way round. It was too hot to go anywhere quickly or even directly.

The park was crowded with games of football, parked prams, sunbathers draped over the greens. Patients sat outside the hospital on Orphan Drive beside the park. Around the lake, fishermen sat by transistor radios and whipped the air with hooks. Beyond the lake, model boats snarled across the shallow circular pool. I stopped to watch their patterns on the water, and caught sight of an object in the shelter.

At first I thought it was an old grey sack that someone had dumped on the bench. Perhaps it held rubbish – sticks that gave parts of it an angular look. Then I saw that the sack was an indeterminate stained garment, which might have been a mackintosh or raincoat of some kind. What I had vaguely assumed to be an ancient shopping bag, resting next to the sack, displayed a ragged patch of flesh and the dull gleam of an eye.

Exposed to daylight, he looked even more dismaying: so huge and still, less stupefied than dormant. The presence of the boatmen with their remote-control boxes reassured me. I ambled past the allotments to Pringle Street, where a terraced house was the editorial office of the *Bugle*.

Our copies were on the way, said Chrissie Maher the editor, and insisted on making me a cup of tea. She seemed a little upset when, having gulped the tea, I hurried out into the rain. Perhaps it was rude of me not to wait until the rain had stopped – but on this parched day I wanted to make the most of it, to bathe my face and my bare arms in the onslaught, gasping almost hysterically.

By the time I had passed the allotments, where cabbages

rattled like toy machine-guns, the downpour was too heavy even for me. The park provided little cover; the trees let fall their own belated storms, miniature but drenching. The nearest shelter was by the pool, which had been abandoned to its web of ripples. I ran down the slippery tarmac hill, splashing through puddles, trying to blink away rain, hoping there would be room in the shelter.

There was plenty of room, both because the rain reached easily into the depths of the brick shed and because the shelter was not entirely empty. He lay as I had seen him, face upturned within the sodden Balaclava. Had the boatmen avoided looking closely at him? Raindrops struck his unblinking eyes and trickled over the patch of flesh.

I hadn't seen death before. I stood shivering and fascinated in the rain. I needn't be scared of him now. He'd stuffed himself into the grey coat until it split in several places; through the rents I glimpsed what might have been dark cloth or discoloured hairy flesh. Above him, on the shelter, were graffiti which at last I saw were not his name at all, but the names of three boys: MACK TOSH WILLY. They were partly erased, which no doubt was why one's mind tended to fill the gap.

I had to keep glancing at him. He grew more and more difficult to ignore; his presence was intensifying. His shapelessness, the rents in his coat, made me think of an old bag of washing, decayed and mouldy. His hand lurked in his sleeve; beside it, amid a scattering of Coca-Cola caps, lay fragments of the bottle whose contents had perhaps killed him. Rain roared on the dull green roof of the shelter; his staring eyes glistened and dripped. Suddenly I was frightened. I ran blindly home.

'There's someone dead in the park,' I gasped. 'The man who chases everyone.'

'Look at you!' my mother cried. 'Do you want pneumonia? Just you get out of those wet things this instant!'

Eventually I had a chance to repeat my news. By this

time the rain had stopped. 'Well, don't be telling us,' my father said. 'Tell the police. They're just across the road.'

Did he think I had exaggerated a drunk into a corpse? He looked surprised when I hurried to the police station. But I couldn't miss the chance to venture in there – I believed that elder brothers of some of my schoolmates had been taken into the station and hadn't come out for years.

Beside a window which might have belonged to a ticket office was a bell you rang to make the window's partition slide back and display a policeman. He frowned down at me. What was my name? What had I been doing in the park? Who had I been with? When a second head appeared beside him he said reluctantly 'He thinks someone's passed out in the park.'

A blue and white Mini called for me at the police station, like a taxi; on the roof a red sign said POLICE. People glanced in at me as though I were on my way to prison. Perhaps I was: suppose Mackintosh Willy had woken up and gone? How long a sentence did you get for lying? False diamonds sparkled on the grass and in the trees. I wished I'd persuaded my father to tell the police.

As the car halted, I saw the grey bulk in the shelter. The driver strode, stiff with dignity, to peer at it. 'My God,' I heard him say in disgust.

Did he know Mackintosh Willy? Perhaps, but that wasn't the point. 'Look at this,' he said to his colleague. 'Ever see a corpse with pennies on the eyes? Just look at this, then. See what someone thought was a joke.'

He looked shocked, sickened. He was blocking my view as he demanded 'Did you do this?'

His white-faced anger, and my incomprehension, made me speechless. But his colleague said 'It wouldn't be him. He wouldn't come and tell us afterwards, would he?'

As I tried to peer past them he said 'Go on home, now. Go on.' His gentleness seemed threatening. Suddenly frightened, I ran home through the park.

For a while I avoided the shelter. I had no reason to go near, except on the way home from school. Sometimes I used to see schoolmates tormenting Mackintosh Willy; sometimes, at a distance, I had joined them. Now the shelter yawned emptily, baring its dim bench. The dark pool stirred, disturbing the green beards of the stone margin. My main reason for avoiding the park was that there was nobody with whom to go.

Living on the main road was the trouble. I belonged to none of the side streets, where they played football among parked cars or chased through the back alleys. I was never invited to street parties. I felt like an outsider, particularly when I had to pass the groups of teenagers who sat on the railings above the pedestrian subway, lazily swinging their legs, waiting to pounce. I stayed at home, in the flat above the newsagent's, when I could, and read everything in the shop. But I grew frustrated: I did enough reading at school. All this was why I welcomed Mark. He could save me from my isolation.

Not that we became friends immediately. He was my parents' latest paperboy. For several days we examined each other warily. He was taller than me, which was intimidating, but seemed unsure how to arrange his lankiness. Eventually he said 'What're you reading?'

He sounded as though reading was a waste of time. 'A book,' I retorted.

At last, when I'd let him see that it was Mickey Spillane, he said 'Can I read it after you?'

'It isn't mine. It's the shop's.'

'All right, so I'll buy it.' He did so at once, paying my father. He was certainly wealthier than me. When my resentment of his gesture had cooled somewhat, I realised that he was letting me finish what was now his book. I dawdled over it to make him complain, but he never did. Perhaps he might be worth knowing.

My instinct was accurate: he proved to be generous –

not only with money, though his father made plenty of that in home improvements, but also in introducing me to his friends. Quite soon I had my place in the tribe at the top of the pedestrian subway, though secretly I was glad that we never exchanged more than ritual insults with the other gangs. Perhaps the police station looming in the background restrained hostilities.

Mark was generous too with his ideas. Although Ben, a burly lad, was nominal leader of the gang, it was Mark who suggested most of our activities. Had he taken to delivering papers to save himself from boredom – or, as I wondered afterwards, to distract himself from his thoughts? It was Mark who brought his skates so that we could brave the slope of the pedestrian subway, who let us ride his bicycle around the side streets, who found ways into derelict houses, who brought his transistor radio so that we could hear the first Beatles records as the traffic passed unheeding on West Derby Road. But was all this a means of distracting us from the park?

No doubt it was inevitable that Ben resented his supremacy. Perhaps he deduced, in his slow and stolid way, that Mark disliked the park. Certainly he hit upon the ideal method to challenge him.

It was a hot summer evening. By then I was thirteen. Dust and fumes drifted in the wakes of cars; wagons clattered repetitively across the railway bridge. We lolled about the pavement, kicking Coca-Cola caps. Suddenly Ben said 'I know something we can do.'

We trooped after him, dodging an aggressive gang of taxis, towards the police station. He might have meant us to play some trick there; when he swaggered past, I'm sure everyone was relieved – everyone except Mark, for Ben was leading us onto Orphan Drive.

Heat shivered above the tarmac. Beside us in the park, twilight gathered beneath the trees, which stirred stealthily. The island in the lake creaked with ducks; swollen litter

31

drifted sluggishly, or tried to climb the bank. I could sense Mark's nervousness. He had turned his radio louder; a misshapen Elvis Presley blundered out of the static, then sank back into incoherence as a neighbourhood waveband seeped into his voice. Why was Mark on edge? I could see only the dimming sky, trees on the far side of the lake diluted by haze, the gleam of bottle caps like eyes atop a floating mound of litter, the glittering of broken bottles in the lawns.

We passed the locked ice-cream kiosk. Ben was heading for the circular pool, whose margin was surrounded by a fluorescent orange tape tied between iron poles, a makeshift fence. I felt Mark's hesitation, as though he were a scared dog dragged by a lead. The lead was pride: he couldn't show fear, especially when none of us knew Ben's plan.

A new concrete path had been laid around the pool. 'We'll write our names in that,' Ben said.

The dark pool swayed, as though trying to douse reflected lights. Black clouds spread over the sky and loomed in the pool; the threat of a storm lurked behind us. The brick shelter was very dim, and looked cavernous. I strode to the orange fence, not wanting to be last, and poked the concrete with my toe. 'We can't,' I said; for some reason I felt relieved. 'It's set.'

Someone had been there before us, before the concrete had hardened. Footprints led from the dark shelter towards us. As they advanced, they faded, no doubt because the concrete had been setting. They looked as though the man had suffered from a limp.

When I pointed them out. Mark flinched, for we heard the radio swing wide of comprehensibility. 'What's up with you?' Ben demanded.

'Nothing.'

'It's getting dark,' I said, not as an answer but to coax everyone back towards the main road. But my remark inspired Ben; contempt grew in his eyes. 'I know what it is,' he said, gesturing at Mark. 'This is where he used to be scared.'

'Who was scared? I wasn't bloody scared.'

'Not much you weren't. You didn't look it,' Ben scoffed, and told us 'Old Willy used to chase him all round the pool. He used to hate him, did old Willy. Mark used to run away from him. I never. I wasn't scared.'

'You watch who you're calling scared. If you'd seen what I did to that old bastard – '

Perhaps the movements around us silenced him. Our surroundings were crowded with dark shifting: the sky unfurled darkness, muddy shapes rushed at us in the pool, a shadow huddled restlessly in one corner of the shelter. But Ben wasn't impressed by the drooping boast. 'Go on,' he sneered. 'You're scared now. Bet you wouldn't dare go in his shelter.'

'Who wouldn't? You watch it, you!'

'Go on then. Let's see you do it.'

We must all have been aware of Mark's fear. His whole body was stiff as a puppet's. I was ready to intervene – to say, lying, that the police were near – when he gave a shrug of despair and stepped forward. Climbing gingerly over the tape as though it were electrified, he advanced onto the concrete.

He strode towards the shelter. He had turned the radio full on; I could hear nothing else, only watch the shifting of dim shapes deep in the reflected sky, watch Mark stepping in the footprints for bravado. They swallowed his feet. He was nearly at the shelter when I saw him glance at the radio.

The song had slipped awry again; another waveband seeped in, a blurred muttering. I thought it must be Mark's infectious nervousness that made me hear it forming into words. 'Come on, son. Let's have a look at you.' But why shouldn't the words have been real, fragments of a radio play?

Mark was still walking, his gaze held by the radio. He seemed almost hypnotised; otherwise he would surely have flinched back from the huddled shadow which surged forward from the corner by the bench, even though it must have been the shadow of a cloud.

As his foot touched the shelter I called nervously 'Come on, Mark. Let's go and skate.' I felt as though I'd saved him. But when he came hurrying back, he refused to look at me or at anyone else.

For the next few days he hardly spoke to me. Perhaps he thought of avoiding my parents' shop. Certainly he stayed away from the gang – which turned out to be all to the good, for Ben, robbed of Mark's ideas, could think only of shoplifting. They were soon caught, for they weren't very skilful. After that my father had doubts about Mark, but Mark had always been scrupulously honest in deliveries; after some reflection, my father kept him on. Eventually Mark began to talk to me again, though not about the park.

That was frustrating: I wanted to tell him how the shelter looked now. I still passed it on my way home, though from a different school. Someone had been scrawling on the shelter. That was hardly unusual – graffiti filled the pedestrian subway, and even claimed the ends of streets – but the words were odd, to say the least: like scribbles on the walls of a psychotic's cell, or the gibberish of an invocation. DO THE BASTARD. BOTTLE UP HIS EYES. HOOK THEM OUT. PUSH HIS HEAD IN. Tangled amid them, like chewed bones, gleamed the eroded slashes of MACK TOSH WILLY.

I wasn't as frustrated by the conversational taboo as I might have been, for I'd met my first girlfriend. Kim was her name; she lived in a flat on my block, and because of her parents' trade, seemed always to smell of fish and chips. She obviously looked up to me – for one thing, I'd begun to read for pleasure again, which few of her friends could be bothered attempting. She told me her secrets, which was a new experience for me, strange and rather exciting – as was being seen on West Derby Road with a girl on my arm, any girl. I was happy to ignore the jeers of Ben and cronies.

She loved the park. Often we strolled through,

scattering charitable crumbs to ducks. Most of all she loved to watch the model yachts, when the snarling model motorboats left them alone to glide over the pool. I enjoyed watching too, while holding her warm if rather clammy hand. The breeze carried away her culinary scent. But I couldn't help noticing that the shelter now displayed screaming faces with red bursts for eyes. I have never seen drawings of violence on walls elsewhere.

My relationship with Kim was short-lived. Like most such teenage experiences, our parting was not romantic and poignant, if partings ever are, but harsh and hysterical. It happened one evening as we made our way to the fair that visited Newsham Park each summer.

Across the lake we could hear shrieks that mingled panic and delight as cars on metal poles swung girls into the air, and the blurred roaring of an ancient pop song, like the voice of an enormous radio. On the Ferris wheel, coloured lights sailed up, painting airborne faces. The twilight shone like a Christmas tree; the lights swam in the pool. That was why Kim said 'Let's sit and look first.'

The only bench was in the shelter. Tangles of letters dripped tails of dried paint, like blood; mutilated faces shrieked soundlessly. Still, I thought I could bear the shelter. Sitting with Kim gave me the chance to touch her breasts, such as they were, through the collapsing deceptively large cups of her bra. Tonight she smelled of newspapers, as though she had been wrapped in them for me to take out; she must have been serving at the counter. Nevertheless I kissed her, and ignored the fact that one corner of the shelter was dark as a spider's crevice.

But she had noticed; I felt her shrink away from the corner. Had she noticed more than I had? Or was it her infectious wariness that made the dark beside us look more solid, about to shuffle towards us along the bench? I was uneasy, but the din and the lights of the fairground were reassuring. I determined to make the most of Kim's need for protection, but she pushed my hand away. 'Don't,' she said irritably, and made to stand up.

At that moment I heard a blurred voice. 'Popeye,' it muttered as if to itself; it sounded gleeful. 'Popeye.' Was it part of the fair? It might have been a stallholder's voice, distorted by the uproar, for it said 'I've got something for you.'

The struggles of Kim's hand in mine excited me. 'Let me go,' she was wailing. Because I managed not to be afraid, I was more pleased than dismayed by her fear — and I was eager to let my imagination flourish, for it was better than reading a ghost story. I peered into the dark corner to see what horrors I could imagine.

Then Kim wrenched herself free and ran around the pool. Disappointed and angry, I pursued her. 'Go away,' she cried. 'You're horrible. I never want to speak to you again.' For a while I chased her along the dim paths, but once I began to plead I grew furious with myself. She wasn't worth the embarrassment. I let her go, and returned to the fair, to wander desultorily for a while. When I'd stayed long enough to prevent my parents from wondering why I was home early, I walked home.

I meant to sit in the shelter for a while, to see if anything happened, but someone was already there. I couldn't make out much about him, and didn't like to go closer. He must have been wearing spectacles, for his eyes seemed perfectly circular and gleamed like metal, not like eyes at all.

I quickly forgot that glimpse, for I discovered Kim hadn't been exaggerating: she refused to speak to me. I stalked off to buy fish and chips elsewhere, and decided that I hadn't liked her anyway. My one lingering disappointment, I found glumly, was that I had nobody with whom to go to the fairground. Eventually, when the fair and the school holidays were approaching their end, I said to Mark 'Shall we go to the fair tonight?'

He hesitated, but didn't seem especially wary. 'All right,' he said with the indifference we were beginning to affect about everything.

At sunset the horizon looked like a furnace, and that was how the park felt. Couples rambled sluggishly along the paths; panting dogs splashed in the lake. Between the trees the lights of the fairground shimmered and twinkled, cheap multicoloured stars. As we passed the pool, I noticed that the air was quivering above the footprints in the concrete, and looked darkened, perhaps by dust. Impulsively I said 'What did you do to old Willy?'

'Shut up.' I'd never heard Mark so savage or withdrawn. 'I wish I hadn't done it.'

I might have retorted to his rudeness, but instead I let myself be captured by the fairground, by the glade of light amid the balding rutted green. Couples and gangs roamed, harangued a shade half-heartedly by stallholders. Young children hid their faces in pink candy floss. A siren thin as a Christmas party hooter set the Dodgems running. Mark and I rode a tilting bucket above the fuzzy clamour of music, the splashes of glaring light, the cramped crowd. Secretly I felt a little sick, but the ride seemed to help Mark regain his confidence. Shortly, as we were playing a pinball machine with senile flippers, he said 'Look, there's Lorna and what's her name.'

It took me a while to be sure where he was pointing: at a tall bosomy girl, who probably looked several years older than she was, and a girl of about my height and age, her small bright face sketched with makeup. By this time I was following him eagerly.

The tall girl was Lorna; her friend's name was Carol. We strolled for a while, picking our way over power cables, and Carol and I began to like each other; her scent was sweet, if rather overpowering. As the fair began to close, Mark easily won trinkets at a shooting gallery and presented them to the girls, which helped us to persuade them to meet

37

us on Saturday night. By now Mark never looked towards the shelter – I think not from wariness but because it had ceased to worry him, at least for the moment. I glanced across, and could just distinguish someone pacing unevenly round the pool, as if impatient for a delayed meeting.

If Mark had noticed, would it have made any difference? Not in the long run, I try to believe. But however I rationalise, I know that some of the blame was mine.

We were to meet Lorna and Carol on our side of the park in order to take them to the Carlton Cinema nearby. We arrived late, having taken our time over sprucing ourselves; we didn't want to seem too eager to meet them. Beside the police station, at the entrance to the park, a triangular island of pavement, large enough to contain a spinney of trees, divided the road. The girls were meant to be waiting at the nearest point of the triangle. But the island was deserted except for the caged darkness beneath the trees.

We waited. Shop windows on West Derby Road glared fluorescent green. Behind us trees whispered, creaking. We kept glancing into the park, but the only figure we could see on the dark paths was alone. Eventually, for something to do, we strolled desultorily around the island.

It was I who saw the message first, large letters scrawled on the corner nearest the park. Was it Lorna's or Carol's handwriting? It rather shocked me, for it looked semiliterate. But she must have had to use a stone as a pencil, which couldn't have helped; indeed, some letters had had to be dug out of the moss that coated stretches of the pavement. MARK SEE YOU AT SHELTER, the message said.

I felt him withdraw a little. 'Which shelter?' he muttered.

'I expect they mean the one near the kiosk,' I said to reassure him.

We hurried along Orphan Drive. Above the lamps, patches of foliage shone harshly. Before we reached the pool we crossed the bridge, from which in daylight manna rained down to the ducks, and entered the park. The fair had gone into hibernation; the paths and the mazes of tree-trunks were silent and very dark. Occasional dim movements made me think that we were passing the girls, but the figure that was wandering a nearby path looked far too bulky.

The shelter was at the edge of the main green, near the football pitch. Beyond the green, tower blocks loomed in glaring auras. Each of the four sides of the shelter was an alcove housing a bench. As we peered into each, jeers or curses challenged us.

'I know where they'll be,' Mark said. 'In the one by the bowling-green. That's near where they live.'

But we were closer to the shelter by the pool. Nevertheless I followed him onto the park road. As we turned towards the bowling-green I glanced towards the pool, but the streetlamps dazzled me. I followed him along a narrow path between hedges to the green, and almost tripped over his ankles as he stopped short. The shelter was empty, alone with its view of the decaying Georgian houses on the far side of the bowling-green.

To my surprise and annoyance, he still didn't head for the pool. Instead we made for the disused bandstand hidden in a ring of bushes. Its only tune now was the clink of broken bricks. I was sure the girls wouldn't have called it a shelter, and of course it was deserted. Obese dim bushes hemmed us in. 'Come on,' I said, 'or we'll miss them. They must be by the pool.'

'They won't be there,' he said – stupidly, I thought.

Did I realise how nervous he suddenly was? Perhaps, but it only annoyed me. After all, how else could I meet Carol again? I didn't know her address. 'Oh, all right,' I scoffed, 'if you want us to miss them.'

I saw him stiffen. Perhaps my contempt hurt him more than Ben's had; for one thing, he was older. Before I knew what he intended he was striding towards the pool, so rapidly that I would have had to run to keep up with him – which, given the hostility that had flared between us, I refused to do. I strolled after him rather disdainfully. That was how I came to glimpse movement in one of the islands of dimness between the lamps of the park road. I glanced towards it and saw, several hundred yards away, the girls.

After a pause they responded to my waving – somewhat timidly, I thought. 'There they are,' I called to Mark. He must have been at the pool by now, but I had difficulty in glimpsing him beyond the glare of the lamps. I was beckoning the girls to hurry when I heard his radio blur into speech.

At first I was reminded of a sailor's parrot. 'Aye aye,' it was croaking. The distorted voice sounded cracked, uneven, almost too old to speak. 'You know what I mean, son?' it grated triumphantly. 'Aye aye.' I was growing uneasy, for my mind had begun to interpret the words as 'Eye eye' – when suddenly, dreadfully, I realised Mark hadn't brought his radio.

There might be someone in the shelter with a radio. But I was terrified, I wasn't sure why. I ran towards the pool calling 'Come on, Mark, they're here!' The lamps dazzled me; everything swayed with my running – which was why I couldn't be sure what I saw.

I know I saw Mark at the shelter. He stood just within, confronting darkness. Before I could discern whether anyone else was there, Mark staggered out blindly, hands covering his face, and collapsed into the pool.

Did he drag something with him? Certainly by the time I reached the margin of the light he appeared to be tangled in something, and to be struggling feebly. He was drifting, or being dragged, towards the centre of the pool by a half-submerged heap of litter. At the end of the heap nearest Mark's face was a pale ragged patch in which gleamed two round objects – bottle caps? I could see all this because I was standing helpless, screaming at the girls 'Quick, for Christ's sake! He's drowning!' He was drowning, and I couldn't swim.

'Don't be stupid,' I heard Lorna say. That enraged me so much that I turned from the pool. 'What do you mean?' I cried. 'What do you mean, you stupid bitch?'

'Oh, be like that,' she said haughtily, and refused to say more. But Carol took pity on my hysteria and explained 'It's only three feet deep. He'll never drown in there.'

I wasn't sure that she knew what she was talking about, but that was no excuse for me not to try to rescue him. When I turned to the pool I gasped miserably, for he had vanished – sunk. I could only wade into the muddy water, which engulfed my legs and closed around my waist like ice, ponderously hindering me.

The floor of the pool was fattened with slimy litter. I slithered, terrified of losing my balance. Intuition urged me to head for the centre of the pool. And it was there I found him, as my sluggish kick collided with his ribs.

When I tried to raise him, I discovered that he was pinned down. I had to grope blindly over him in the chill water, feeling how still he was. Something like a swollen cloth bag, very large, lay over his face. I couldn't bear to touch it again, for its contents felt soft and fat. Instead I seized Mark's ankles and managed at last to drag him free. Then I struggled towards the edge of the pool, heaving him by his shoulders, lifting his head above water. His weight was dismaying. Eventually the girls waded out to help me.

But we were too late. When we dumped him on the concrete, his face stayed agape with horror; water lay stagnant in his mouth. I could see nothing wrong with his eyes. Carol grew hysterical, and it was Lorna who ran to the hospital, perhaps in order to get away from the sight of him. I only made Carol worse by demanding why they hadn't waited for us at the shelter; I wanted to feel they were to blame. But she denied they had written the message, and grew more hysterical when I asked why they hadn't waited at the island. The question, or the memory, seemed to frighten her.

I never saw her again. The few newspapers that bothered to report Mark's death gave the verdict 'by misadventure.' The police took a dislike to me after I insisted that there might be somebody else in the pool, for the draining revealed nobody. At least, I thought, whatever was there had gone away. Perhaps I could take some credit for that at least.

But perhaps I was too eager for reassurance. The last time I ventured near the shelter was years ago, one winter night on the way home from school. I had caught sight of a gleam in the depths of the shelter. As I went close, nervously watching both the shelter and the pool, I saw two discs glaring at me from the darkness beside the bench. They were Coca-Cola caps, not eyes at all, and it must have been the wind that set the pool slopping and sent the caps scuttling towards me. What frightened me most as I fled through the dark was that I wouldn't be able to see where I was running if, as I desperately wanted to, I put up my hands to protect my eyes.

The Forbidden

Clive Barker

Like a flawless tragedy, the elegance of whose structure is lost upon those suffering in it, the perfect geometry of the Spector Street Estate was only visible from the air. Walking in its drear canyons, passing through its grimy corridors from one grey concrete rectangle to the next, there was little to seduce the eye or stimulate the imagination. What few saplings had been planted in the quadrangles had long since been mutilated or uprooted; the grass, though tall, resolutely refused a healthy green.

No doubt the estate and its two companion developments had once been an architect's dream. No doubt the city-planners had wept with pleasure at a design which housed three hundred and thirty-six persons per hectare, and still boasted space for a children's playground. Doubtless fortunes and reputations had been built upon Spector Street, and at its opening fine words had been spoken of its being a yardstick by which all future developments would be measured. But the planners – tears wept, words spoken – had left the estate to its own devices; the architects occupied restored Georgian houses at the other end of the city, and probably never set foot here.

They would not have been shamed by the deterioration of the estate even if they had. Their brain-child (they would doubtless argue) was as brilliant as ever: its geometries as precise, its ratios as calculated; it was *people* who had spoiled Spector Street. Nor would they have been wrong in such an accusation. Helen had seldom seen an inner city environment so comprehensively vandalized. Lamps had been shattered and back-yard fences overthrown; cars whose wheels and engines had been removed and chassis then burned, blocked garage facilities. In one courtyard three or four ground-floor maisonettes had been entirely gutted by fire, their windows and doors boarded up with planks and corrugated iron.

More startling still was the graffiti. That was what she had come here to see, encouraged by Archie's talk of the place, and she was not disappointed. It was difficult to believe, staring at the multiple layers of designs, names, obscenities, and dogmas that were scrawled and sprayed on every available brick, that Spector Street was barely three and a half years old. The walls, so recently virgin, were now so profoundly defaced that the Council Cleaning Department could never hope to return them to their former condition. A layer of whitewash to cancel this visual cacophony would only offer the scribes a fresh and yet more tempting surface on which to make their mark.

Helen was in seventh heaven. Every corner she turned offered some fresh material for her thesis: '*Graffiti: the semiotics of urban despair*'. It was a subject which married her two favourite disciplines – sociology and aesthetics – and as she wandered around the estate she began to wonder if there wasn't a book, in addition to her thesis, in the subject. She walked from courtyard to courtyard, copying down a large number of the more interesting scrawlings, and noting their location. Then she went back to the car to collect her camera and tripod and returned to the most fertile of the areas, to make a thorough visual record of the walls.

It was a chilly business. She was not an expert photographer, and the late October sky was in full flight, shifting the light on the bricks from one moment to the next. As she adjusted and re-adjusted the exposure to compensate for the light changes, her fingers steadily became clumsier, her temper correspondingly thinner. But she struggled on, the idle curiosity of passers-by notwithstanding. There were so many designs to document. She reminded herself that her present discomfort would be amply repaid when she showed the slides to Trevor, whose doubt of the project's validity had been perfectly apparent from the beginning.

'The writing on the wall?' he'd said, half smiling in that irritating fashion of his, 'It's been done a hundred times.'

This was true, of course; and yet not. There certainly were learned works on graffiti, chock full of sociological jargon: *cultural disenfranchisement; urban alienation.* But she flattered herself that *she* might find something amongst this litter of scrawlings that previous analysts had not: some unifying convention perhaps, that she could use as the lynch-pin of her thesis. Only a vigorous cataloguing and cross-referencing of the phrases and images before her would reveal such a correspondence; hence the importance of this photographic study. So many hands had worked here; so many minds left their mark, however casually: if she could find some pattern, some predominant motive, or *motif*, the thesis would be guaranteed some serious attentions, and so, in turn, would she.

'What are you doing?' a voice from behind her asked.

She turned from her calculations to see a young woman with a pushchair on the pavement behind her. She looked weary, Helen thought, and pinched by the cold. The child in the pushchair was mewling, his grimy fingers clutching an orange lollipop and the wrapping from a chocolate bar. The bulk of the chocolate, and the remains of previous jujubes, was displayed down the front of his coat.

Helen offered a thin smile to the woman; she looked in need if it.

'I'm photographing the walls,' she said in answer to the initial enquiry, though surely this was perfectly apparent.

The woman – though she could barely be twenty – Helen judged, said: 'You mean the filth?'

'The writing and the pictures,' Helen said. Then: 'Yes. The filth.'

'You from the Council?'

'No, the University.'

'It's bloody disgusting,' the woman said. 'The way they do that. It's not just kids, either.'

'No?'

'Grown men. Grown men, too. They don't give a damn. Do it in broad daylight. You see 'em... broad daylight.' She glanced down at the child, who was sharpening his lollipop on the ground. 'Kerry!' she snapped, but the boy took no notice. 'Are they going to wipe it off?' she asked Helen.

'I don't know,' Helen said, and reiterated: 'I'm from the University.'

'Oh,' the woman replied, as if this was new information, 'so you're nothing to do with the Council?'

'No.'

'Some of it's obscene, isn't it?; really dirty. Makes me embarrassed to see some of the things they draw.'

Helen nodded, casting an eye at the boy in the pushchair. Kerry had decided to put his sweet in his ear for safe-keeping.

'Don't do that!' his mother told him, and leaned over to slap the child's hand. The blow, which was negligible, began the child bawling. Helen took the opportunity to return to her camera. But the woman still desired to talk. 'It's not just on the outside, neither,' she commented.

'I beg your pardon?' Helen said.

'They break into the flats when they go empty. The Council tried to board them up, but it does no good. They break in anyway. Use them as toilets, and write more filth on the walls. They light fires too. Then nobody can move back in.'

The description piqued Helen's curiosity. Would the graffiti on the *inside* walls be substantially different from the public displays? It was certainly worth an investigation.

'Are there any places you know of around here like that?'

'Empty flats, you mean?'

'With graffiti.'

'Just by us, there's one or two,' the woman volunteered. 'I'm in Butts' Court.'

'Maybe you could show me?' Helen asked.

The woman shrugged.

'By the way, my name's Helen Buchanan.'

'Anne-Marie,' the mother replied.

'I'd be very grateful if you could point me to one of those empty flats.'

Anne-Marie was baffled by Helen's enthusiasm, and made no attempt to disguise it, but she shrugged again and said: 'There's nothing much to see. Only more of the same stuff.'

Helen gathered up her equipment and they walked side by side through the intersecting corridors between one square and the next. Though the estate was low-rise, each court only five storeys high, the effect of each quadrangle was horribly claustrophobic. The walkways and staircases were a thief's dream, rife with blind corners and ill-lit tunnels. The rubbish-dumping facilities — chutes from the upper floors down which bags of refuse could be pitched — had long since been sealed up, thanks to their efficiency as fire-traps. Now plastic bags of refuse were piled high in the corridors, many torn open by the roaming dogs, their contents strewn across the ground. The smell, even in the cold weather, was unpleasant. In high summer it must have been overpowering.

'I'm over the other side,' Anne-Marie said, pointing across the quadrangle. 'The one with the yellow door.' She then pointed along the opposite side of the court. 'Five or six maisonettes from the far end,' she said. 'There's two of them been emptied out. Few weeks now. One of the families has moved into Ruskin Court; the other did a bunk in the middle of the night.'

With that, she turned her back on Helen and wheeled

Kerry, who had taken to trailing spittle from the side of his pushchair, around the side of the square.

'Thank you,' Helen called after her. Anne-Marie glanced over her shoulder briefly, but did not reply. Appetite whetted, Helen made her way along the row of ground floor maisonettes, many of which, though inhabited, showed little sign of being so. Their curtains were closely drawn; there were no milk-bottles on the doorsteps, nor children's toys left where they had been played with. Nothing, in fact, of *life* here. There *was* more graffiti however, sprayed, shockingly, on the doors of occupied houses. She granted the scrawlings only a casual perusal, in part because she feared one of the doors opening as she examined a choice obscenity sprayed upon it, but more because she was eager to see what revelations the empty flats ahead might offer.

The malign scent of urine, both fresh and stale, welcomed her at the threshold of number 14, and beneath that the smell of burnt paint and plastic. She hesitated for fully ten seconds, wondering if stepping into the maisonette was a wise move. The territory of the estate behind her was indisputably foreign, sealed off in its own misery, but the rooms in front of her were more intimidating still: a dark maze which her eyes could barely penetrate. But when her courage faltered she thought of Trevor, and how badly she wanted to silence his condescension. So thinking, she advanced into the place deliberately kicking a piece of charred timber aside as she did so, in the hope that she would alert any tenant into showing himself.

There was no sound of occupancy however. Gaining confidence, she began to explore the front room of the maisonette which had been − to judge by the remains of a disembowelled sofa in one corner and the sodden carpet underfoot − a living room. The pale-green walls were, as Anne-Marie had promised, extensively defaced, both by minor scribblers − content to work in pen , or even more crudely in sofa charcoal − and by those with aspirations to public works, who had sprayed the walls in half a dozen colours.

Some of the comments were of interest, though many she had already seen on the walls outside. Familiar names and couplings repeated themselves. Though she had never set eyes on these individuals she knew how badly Fabian J. (A.OK!) wanted to deflower Michelle; and that Michelle, in her turn, had the hots for somebody called Mr Sheen. Here, as elsewhere, a man called White Rat boasted of his endowment, and the return of the Syllabub Brothers was promised in red paint. One or two of the pictures accompanying, or at least adjacent to, these phrases were of particular interest. An almost emblematic simplicity informed them. Beside the word *Christos* was a stick man with his hair radiating from his head like spines, and other heads impaled on each spine. Close by was an image of intercourse so brutally reduced that at first Helen took it to illustrate a knife plunging into a sightless eye. But fascinating as the images were, the room was too gloomy for her film and she had neglected to bring a flash. If she wanted a reliable record of these discoveries she would have to come again, and for now be content with a simple exploration of the premises.

The maisonette wasn't that large, but the windows had been boarded up throughout, and as she moved further from the front door the dubious light petered out altogether. The smell of urine, which had been strong at the door, intensified too, until by the time she reached the back of the living-room and stepped along a short corridor into another room beyond, it was cloying as incense. This room, being furthest from the front door, was also the darkest, and she had to wait a few moments in the cluttered gloom to allow her eyes to become useful. This, she guessed, had been the bedroom. What little furniture the residents had left behind them had been smashed to smithereens. Only the mattress had been left relatively untouched, dumped in the corner of the room amongst a wretched litter of blankets, newspapers, and pieces of crockery.

Outside, the sun found its way between the clouds, and two or three shafts of sunlight slipped between the boards nailed across the bedroom window and pierced the room like annunciations, scoring the opposite wall with bright lines. Here, the graffitists had been busy once more: the usual clamour of love-letters and threats. She scanned the wall quickly, and as she did so her eye was led by the beams of light across the room to the wall which contained the door she had stepped through.

Here, the artists had also been at work, but had produced an image the like of which she had not seen anywhere else. Using the door, which was centrally placed in the wall, as a mouth, the artists had sprayed a single, vast head on to the stripped plaster. The painting was more adroit than most she had seen, rife with detail that lent the image an unsettling veracity. The cheekbones jutting through skin the colour of buttermilk; the teeth – sharpened to irregular points – all converging on the door. The sitter's eyes were, owing to the room's low ceiling, set mere inches above the upper lip, but this physical adjustment only lent force to the image, giving the impression that he had thrown his head back. Knotted strands of his hair snaked from his scalp across the ceiling.

Was it a portrait? There was something naggingly *specific* in the details of the brows and the lines around the wide mouth; in the careful picturing of those vicious teeth. A nightmare certainly: a facsimile, perhaps, of something from a heroin fugue. Whatever its origins, it was potent. Even the illusion of door-as-mouth worked. The short passageway between living-room and bedroom offered a passable throat, with a tattered lamp in lieu of tonsils. Beyond the gullet, the day burned white in the nightmare's belly. The whole effect brought to mind a ghost train painting. The same heroic deformity, the same unashamed intention to scare. And it worked; she stood in the bedroom almost stupefied by the picture, its red-rimmed eyes fixing her mercilessly. Tomorrow, she determined, she would come here again, this time with high-speed film and a flash to illuminate the masterwork.

As she prepared to leave the sun went in, and the bands of light faded. She glanced over her shoulder at the boarded windows, and saw for the first time that one four-word slogan had been sprayed on the wall beneath them.

'*Sweets to the sweet*,' it read. She was familiar with the quote, but not with its source. Was it a profession of love? If so, it was an odd location for such an avowal. Despite the mattress in the corner, and the relative privacy of this room, she could not imagine the intended reader of such words ever stepping in here to receive her bouquet. No adolescent lovers, however heated, would lie down here to play at mothers and fathers; not under the gaze of the terror on the wall. She crossed to examine the writing. The paint looked to be the same shade of pink as had been used to colour the gums of the screaming man; perhaps the same hand?

Behind her, a noise. She turned so quickly she almost tripped over the blanket-strewn mattress.

'Who – ?'

At the other end of the gullet, in the living-room, was a scab-kneed boy of six or seven. He stared at Helen, eyes glittering in the half-light as if waiting for a cue.

'Yes?' she said.

'Anne-Marie says do you want a cup of tea?' he declared without pause or intonation.

Her conversation with the woman seemed hours past. She was grateful for the invitation however. The damp in the maisonette had chilled her.

'Yes…' she said to the boy. 'Yes please.'

The child didn't move, but simply stared on at her.

'Are you going to lead the way?' she asked him.

'If you want,' he replied, unable to raise a trace of enthusiasm.

51

'I'd like that.'

'You taking photographs?' he asked.

'Yes. Yes, I am. But not in here.'

'Why not?'

'It's too dark,' she told him.

'Don't it work in the dark?' he wanted to know.

'No.'

The boy nodded at this, as if the information fitted well into his scheme of things, and about turned without another word, clearly expecting Helen to follow.

If she had been taciturn in the street, Anne-Marie was anything but in the privacy of her own kitchen. Gone was the guarded curiosity, to be replaced by a stream of lively chatter and a constant scurrying between half a dozen minor domestic tasks, like a juggler keeping several plates spinning simultaneously. Helen watched this balancing act with some admiration; her own domestic skills were negligible. At last, the meandering conversation turned back to the subject that had brought Helen here.

'Them photographs,' Anne-Marie said, 'why'd you want to take them?'

'I'm writing about graffiti. The photos will illustrate my thesis.'

'It's not very pretty.'

'No, you're right, it isn't. But I find it interesting.'

Anne-Marie shook her head. 'I hate the whole estate,' she said. 'It's not safe here. People getting robbed on their own doorsteps. Kids setting fire to the rubbish day in, day out. Last summer we had the fire brigade here two, three times a day, 'til they sealed them chutes off. Now people just dump the bags in the passageways, and that attracts rats.'

'Do you live here alone?'

'Yes,' she said, 'since Davey walked out.'

'That your husband?'

'He was Kerry's father, but we weren't never married.

We lived together two years, you know. We had some good times. Then he just upped and went off one day when I was at me Mam's with Kerry'. She peered into her tea-cup. 'I'm better off without him,' she said. 'But you get scared sometimes. Want some more tea?'

'I don't think I've got time.'

'Just a cup,' Anne-Marie said, already up and unplugging the electric kettle to take it across for a re-fill. As she was about to turn on the tap she saw something on the draining board, and drove her thumb down, grinding it out. 'Got you, you bugger,' she said, then turned to Helen: 'We got these bloody ants.'

'Ants?'

'Whole estate's infected. From Egypt, they are: pharaoh ants, they're called. Little brown sods. They breed in the central heating ducts, you see; that way they get into all the flats. Place is plagued with them.'

This unlikely exoticism (ants from Egypt?) struck Helen as comical, but she said nothing. Anne-Marie was staring out of the kitchen window and into the back-yard.

'You should tell them –' she said, though Helen wasn't certain whom she was being instructed to tell, 'tell them that ordinary people can't even walk the streets any longer –'

'Is it really so bad?' Helen said, frankly tiring of this catalogue of misfortunes.

Anne-Marie turned from the sink and looked at her hard.

'We've had murders here, 'she said.

'Really?'

'We had one in the summer. An old man he was, from Ruskin. That's just next door. I didn't know him, but he was a friend of the sister of the woman next door. I forget his name.'

'And he was murdered?'

'Cut to ribbons in his own front room. They didn't find him for almost a week.'

'What about his neighbours? Didn't they notice his absence?'

Anne-Marie shrugged, as if the most important pieces of information – the murder and the man's isolation – had been exchanged, and any further enquiries into the problem were irrelevant. But Helen pressed the point.

'Seems strange to me,' she said.

Anne-Marie plugged in the filled kettle. 'Well, it happened,' she replied, unmoved.

'I'm not saying it didn't, I just –'

'His eyes had been taken out,' she said, before Helen could voice any further doubts.

Helen winced. 'No,' she said, under her breath.

'That's the truth.' Anne-Marie said. 'And that wasn't all'd been done to him.' She paused, for effect, then went on: 'You wonder what kind of person's capable of doing things like that, don't you? You wonder.' Helen nodded. She was thinking precisely the same thing.

'Did they ever find the man responsible?'

Anne-Marie snorted her disparagement. 'Police don't give a damn what happens here. They keep off the estate as much as possible. When they do patrol all they do is pick up kids for getting drunk and that. They're afraid, you see. That's why they keep clear.'

'Of this killer?'

'Maybe,' Anne-Marie replied. Then: 'He had a hook.'

'A hook?'

'The man what done it. He had a hook, like Jack the Ripper.'

Helen was no expert on murder, but she felt certain that the Ripper hadn't boasted a hook. It seemed churlish to question the truth of Anne-Marie's story however; though she silently wondered how much of this – the eyes taken out, the body rotting in the flat, the hook – was elaboration. The most scrupulous of reporters was surely tempted to embellish a story once in a while.

Anne-Marie had poured herself another cup of tea, and was about to do the same for her guest.

'No thank you,' Helen said. 'I really should go.'

'You married?' Anne-Marie asked, out of the blue.

'Yes. To a lecturer from the University.'

'What's his name?'

'Trevor.'

Anne-Marie put two heaped spoonfuls of sugar into her cup of tea.

'Will you be coming back?' she asked.

'Yes, I hope to. Later in the week. I want to take some photographs of the pictures in the maisonette across the court.'

'Well, call in.'

'I shall. And thank you for your help.'

'That's all right,' Anne-Marie replied. 'You've got to tell somebody, haven't you?'

'The man apparently had a hook instead of a hand.'

Trevor looked up from his plate of *tagliatelle con prosciutto*.

'Beg your pardon?'

Helen had been at pains to keep her recounting of this story as uncoloured by her own response as she could. She was interested to know what Trevor would make of it, and she knew that if she once signalled her own stance he would instinctively take an opposing view out of plain bloody-mindedness.

'He had a hook,' she repeated, without inflexion.

Trevor put down his fork, and plucked at his nose, sniffing. 'I didn't read anything about this,' he said.

'You don't look at the local press,' Helen returned. 'Neither of us do. Maybe it never made any of the nationals.'

'"Geriatric Murdered By Hook-Handed Maniac"?' Trevor said, savouring the hyperbole. 'I would have thought it very newsworthy. When was all of this supposed to have happened?'

CLIVE BARKER

'Sometime last summer. Maybe we were in Ireland.'

'Maybe,' said Trevor, taking up his fork again. Bending to his food, the polished lens of his spectacles reflected only the plate of pasta and chopped ham in front of him, not his eyes.

'Why do you say *maybe*?' Helen prodded.

'It doesn't sound quite right,' he said. 'In fact it sounds bloody preposterous.'

'You don't believe it?' Helen said.

Trevor looked up from his food, tongue rescuing a speck of *tagliatelle* from the corner of his mouth. His face had relaxed into that non-committal expression of his – the same face he wore, no doubt, when listening to his students. 'Do *you* believe it?' he asked Helen. It was a favourite time-gaining device of his, another seminar trick, to question the questioner.

'I'm not certain,' Helen replied, too concerned to find some solid ground in this sea of doubts to waste energy scoring points.

'All right, forget the tale –' Trevor said, deserting his food for another glass of red wine, '– what about the teller? Did you trust her?'

Helen pictured Anne-Marie's earnest expression as she told the story of the old man's murder. 'Yes,' she said. 'Yes; I think I would have known if she'd been lying to me.'

'So why's it so important, anyhow? I mean, whether she's lying or not, what the fuck does it matter?'

It was a reasonable question, if irritatingly put. Why *did* it matter? Was it that she wanted to have her worst feelings about Spector Street proved false? That such an estate be filthy, be hopeless, be a dump where the undesirable and the disadvantaged were tucked out of public view – all that was a liberal commonplace, and she accepted it as an unpalatable social reality. But the story of the old man's murder and mutilation was something other. An image of violent death that, once with her, refused to part from her company.

56

She realized, to her chagrin, that this confusion was plain on her face, and that Trevor, watching her across the table, was not a little entertained by it.

'If it bothers you so much,' he said, 'why don't you go back there and ask around, instead of playing believe-in-it-or-not over dinner?'

She couldn't help but rise to his remark. 'I thought you liked guessing games,' she said.

He threw her a sullen look.

'Wrong again.'

The suggestion that she investigate was not a bad one, though doubtless he had ulterior motives for offering it. She viewed Trevor less charitably day by day. What she had once thought in him a fierce commitment to debate she now recognized as mere power-play. He argued, not for the thrill of dialectic, but because he was pathologically competitive. She had seen him, time and again, take up attitudes she knew he did not espouse, simply to spill blood. Nor, more's the pity, was he alone in this sport. Academe was one of the last strongholds of the professional time-waster. On occasion their circle seemed entirely dominated by educated fools, lost in a wasteland of stale rhetoric and hollow commitment.

From one wasteland to another. She returned to Spector Street the following day, armed with a flashgun in addition to her tripod and high-sensitive film. The wind was up today, and it was Arctic, more furious still for being trapped in the maze of passageways and courts. She made her way to number 14, and spent the next hour in its befouled confines, meticulously photographing both the bedroom and the living-room walls. She had half expected the impact of the head in the bedroom to be dulled by re-acquaintance; it was not. Though she struggled to capture its scale and detail as best she could, she knew the photographs would be at best a dim echo of its perpetual howl.

Much of its power lay in its context, of course. That

such an image might be stumbled upon in surroundings so drab, so conspicuously lacking in mystery, was akin to finding an icon on a rubbish-heap: a gleaming symbol of transcendence from a world of toil and decay into some darker but more tremendous realm. She was painfully aware that the intensity of her response probably defied her articulation. Her vocabulary was analytic, replete with buzz-words and academic terminology, but woefully impoverished when it came to evocation. The photographs, pale as they would be, would, she hoped, at least hint at the potency of this picture, even if they couldn't conjure the way it froze the bowels.

When she emerged from the maisonette the wind was as uncharitable as ever, but the boy waiting outside – the same child as had attended upon her yesterday – was dressed as if for spring weather. He grimaced in his effort to keep the shudders at bay.

'Hello,' Helen said.

'I waited,' the child announced.

'Waited?'

'Anne-Marie said you'd come back.'

'I wasn't planning to come until later in the week,' Helen said. 'You might have waited a long time.'

The boy's grimace relaxed a notch. 'It's all right,' he said, 'I've got nothing to do.'

'What about school?'

'Don't like it,' the boy replied, as if unobliged to be educated if it wasn't to his taste.

'I see,' said Helen, and began to walk down the side of the quadrangle. The boy followed. On the patch of grass at the centre of the quadrangle several chairs and two or three dead saplings had been piled.

'What's this?' she said, half to herself.

'Bonfire Night,' the boy informed her. 'Next week.'

'Of course.'

'You going to see Anne-Marie?' he asked.

'Yes.'

'She's not in.'

'Oh. Are you sure?'

'Yeah.'

'Well perhaps *you* can help me...' She stopped and turned to face the child; smooth sacs of fatigue hung beneath his eyes. 'I heard about an old man who was murdered near here,' she said to him. 'In the summer. Do you know anything about that?'

'No.'

'Nothing at all? You don't remember anybody getting killed?'

'No,' the boy said again, with impressive finality. 'I don't remember.'

'Well, thank you anyway.'

This time when she retraced her steps back to the car, the boy didn't follow. But as she turned the corner out of the quadrangle she glanced back to see him standing on the spot where she'd left him, staring after her as if she were a madwoman.

By the time she had reached the car and packed the photographic equipment into the boot there were specks of rain in the wind, and she was sorely tempted to forget she'd ever heard Anne-Marie's story and make her way home, where the coffee would be warm even if the welcome wasn't. But she needed an answer to the question Trevor had put the previous night. Do *you* believe it?, he'd asked when she'd told him the story. She hadn't known how to answer then, and she still didn't. Perhaps (why did she sense this?) the terminology of verifiable truth was redundant here; perhaps the final answer to his question was not an answer at all, only another question. If so; so. She had to find out.

Ruskin Court was as forlorn as its fellows, if not more so. It didn't even boast a bonfire. On the third floor balcony a woman was taking washing in before the rain broke; on the grass in the centre of the quadrangle two dogs were absent-mindedly rutting, the fuckee staring up at the blank sky. As she walked along the empty pavement she set her face determinedly; a purposeful look, Bernadette had once said, deterred attack. When she caught sight of the two women talking at the far end of the court she crossed over to them hurriedly, grateful for their presence.

'Excuse me?'

The women, both in middle-age, ceased their animated exchange and looked her over.

'I wonder if you can help me?'

She could feel their appraisal, and their distrust; they went undisguised. One of the pair, her face florid, said plainly: 'What do you want?'

Helen suddenly felt bereft of the least power to charm. What was she to say to these two that wouldn't make her motives appear ghoulish? 'I was told... she began, and then stumbled, aware that she would get no assistance from either woman. '... I was told there'd been a murder near here. Is that right?'

The florid woman raised eyebrows so plucked they were barely visible. 'Murder?' she said.

'Are you from the press?' the other woman enquired. The years had soured her features beyond sweetening. Her small mouth was deeply lined; her hair, which had been dyed brunette, showed a half-inch of grey in her roots.

'No, I'm not from the press,' Helen said, 'I'm a friend of Anne-Marie's, in Butts' Court.' This claim of *friend* stretched the truth, but it seemed to mellow the women somewhat.

'Visiting are you?' the florid woman asked.

'In a manner of speaking –'

'You missed the warm spell –'

'Anne-Marie was telling me about somebody who'd been murdered here, during the summer. I was curious about it.'

'Is that right?'

'– do you know anything about it?'

'Lots of things go on around here,' said the second woman. 'You don't know the half of it.'

'So it's true,' Helen said.

'They had to close the toilets,' the first woman put in.

'That's right. They did,' the other said.

'The toilets?' Helen said. What had this to do with the old man's death?

'It was terrible,' the first said. 'Was it your Frank, Josie, who told you about it?'

'No, not Frank,' Josie replied. 'Frank was still at sea. It was Mrs Tyzack.'

The witness established, Josie relinquished the story to her companion, and turned her gaze back upon Helen. The suspicion had not yet died from her eyes.

'This was only the month before last,' Josie said. 'Just about the end of August. It was August, wasn't it?' She looked to the other woman for verification. 'You've got the head for dates, Maureen.'

Maureen looked uncomfortable. 'I forget,' she said, clearly unwilling to offer testimony.

'I'd like to know,' Helen said. Josie, despite her companion's reluctance, was eager to oblige.

'There's some lavatories,' she said, 'outside the shops – you know, public lavatories. I'm not quite sure how it all happened exactly, but there used to be a boy... well, he wasn't a boy really, I mean he was a man of twenty or more, but he was...' she fished for the words, '...mentally subnormal, I suppose you'd say. His mother used to have to take him around like he was a four year old. Anyhow, she let him go into the lavatories while she went to that little supermarket, what's it called?' she turned to Maureen for a prompt, but the other woman just looked back, her disapproval plain. Josie was ungovernable, however. 'Broad daylight, this was,' she said to Helen. 'Middle of the day. Anyhow, the boy went to the toilet, and the mother was in the shop. And after a while, you know how you do, she's busy shopping, she forgets about him, and then she thinks he's been gone a long time...'

At this juncture Maureen couldn't prevent herself from butting in: the accuracy of the story apparently took precedence over her wariness.

'– She got into an argument,' she corrected Josie, 'with the manager. About some bad bacon she'd had from him. That was why she was such a time... '

'I see,' said Helen.

'– Anyway,' said Josie, picking up the tale, 'she finished her shopping and when she came out he still wasn't there –'

'So she asked someone from the supermarket –' Maureen began, but Josie wasn't about to have her narrative snatched back at this vital juncture.

'She asked one of the men from the supermarket –' she repeated over Maureen's interjection, 'to go down into the lavatory and find him.'

'It was terrible,' said Maureen, clearly picturing the atrocity in her mind's eye.

'He was lying on the floor, in a pool of blood.'

'Murdered?'

Josie shook her head. 'He'd have been better off dead. He'd been attacked with a razor –' she let this piece of information sink in before delivering the *coup de grace,* '– and they'd cut off his private parts. Just cut them off and flushed them down the toilet. No reason on earth to do it.

'Oh my God.'

'Better off dead,' Josie repeated. 'I mean, they can't mend something like that, can they?'

The appalling tale was rendered worse still by the *sang-froid* of the teller, and by the casual repetition of 'Better off dead'.

'The boy,' Helen said, 'was he able to describe his attackers?'

'No,' said Josie, 'he's practically an imbecile. He can't string more than two words together.'

'And nobody saw anyone go into the lavatory? Or leaving it?'

'People come and go all the time –' Maureen said. This, though it sounded like an adequate explanation, had not been Helen's experience. There was not a great bustle in the quadrangle and passageways; far from it. Perhaps the shopping mall was busier, she reasoned, and might offer adequate cover for such a crime.

'So they haven't found the culprit,' she said.

'No,' Josie replied, her eyes losing their fervour. The crime and its immediate consequences were the nub of this story; she had little or no interest in either the culprit or his capture.

'We're not safe in our own beds,' Maureen observed. 'You ask anyone.'

'Anne-Marie said the same,' Helen replied. 'That's how she came to tell me about the old man. Said he was murdered during the summer, here in Ruskin Court.'

'I do remember something,' Josie said. 'There *was* some talk I heard. An old man, and his dog. He was battered to death, and the dog ended up... I don't know. It certainly wasn't here. It must have been one of the other estates.'

'Are you sure?'

The woman looked offended by this slur on her memory. 'Oh yes,' she said, 'I mean if it had been here, we'd have known the story, wouldn't we?'

Helen thanked the pair for their help and decided to take a stroll around the quadrangle anyway, just to see how many more maisonettes were out of operation here. As in Butts' Court, many of the curtains were drawn and all the doors locked. But then if Spector Street *was* under siege from a maniac capable of the murder and mutilation such as she'd heard described, she was not surprised that the residents took to their homes and stayed there. There was nothing much to see around the court. All the unoccupied maisonettes and flats had been recently sealed, to judge by a litter of nails left on a doorstep by the council workmen. One sight *did* catch her attention however. Scrawled on the paving stones she was walking over – and all but erased by rain and the passage of feet – the same phrase she'd seen in the bedroom of number 14: *Sweets to the sweet.* The words were so benign; why did she seem to sense menace in them? Was it in their excess, perhaps, in the sheer overabundance of sugar upon sugar, honey upon honey?

She walked on, though the rain persisted, and her walkabout gradually led her away from the quadrangles and into the concrete no-man's-land through which she had not previously passed. This was – or had been – the site of the estate's amenities. Here was the children's playground, its metal-framed rides overturned, its sandpit fouled by dogs, its paddling pool empty. And here too were the shops. Several had been boarded up; those that hadn't were dingy and unattractive, their windows protected by heavy wire-mesh.

She walked along the row, and rounded a corner, and there in front of her was a squat brick building. The public lavatory, she guessed, though the signs designating it as such had gone. The iron gates were closed and padlocked. Standing in front of the charmless building, the wind gusting around her legs, she couldn't help but think of what had happened here. Of the man-child, bleeding on the floor, helpless to cry out. It made her queasy even to contemplate it. She turned her thoughts instead to the felon. What would he look like, she wondered, a man capable of such depravities? She tried to make an image of him, but no detail she could conjure carried sufficient force. But then monsters were seldom very terrible once hauled into the plain light of day. As long as this man was known only by his deeds he held untold power over the imagination; but the human truth beneath the terrors would, she knew, be bitterly disappointing. No monster he; just a whey-faced apology for a man more needful of pity than awe.

The next gust of wind brought the rain on more heavily. It was time, she decided, to be done with adventures for the day. Turning her back on the public lavatories she hurried back through the quadrangles to the refuge of the car, the icy rain needling her face to numbness.

The dinner guests looked gratifyingly appalled at the story, and Trevor, to judge by the expression on his face, was furious. It was done now, however; there was no taking it back. Nor could she deny the satisfaction she took in having silenced the inter-departmental babble about the table. It was Bernadette, Trevor's assistant in the History Department, who broke the agonizing hush.

'When was this?'

'During the summer,' Helen told her.

'I don't recall reading about it,' said Archie, much the better for two hours of drinking; it mellowed a tongue which was otherwise fulsome in its self-coruscation.

'Perhaps the police are suppressing it,' Daniel commented.

'Conspiracy?' said Trevor, plainly cynical.

'It's happening all the time,' Daniel shot back.

'Why would they suppress something like this?' Helen said. 'It doesn't make sense.'

'Since when has the police procedure made sense?' Daniel replied.

Bernadette cut in before Helen could answer. 'We don't even bother to read about these things any longer,' she said.

'Speak for yourself,' somebody piped up, but she ignored them and went on:

'We're punch-drunk with violence. We don't see it any longer, even when it's in front of our noses.'

'On the screen every night,' Archie put in, 'Death and disaster in full colour.'

'There's nothing very modern about that,' Trevor said.

'An Elizabethan would have seen death all the time. Public executions were a very popular form of entertainment.'

The table broke into a cacophony of opinions. After two hours of polite gossip the dinner-party had suddenly caught fire. Listening to the debate rage Helen was sorry she hadn't had time to have the photographs processed and printed; the graffiti would have added further fuel to this exhilarating row. It was Purcell, as usual, who was the last to weigh in with his point of view; and – again, as usual – it was devastating.

'Of course, Helen, my sweet –' he began, that affected weariness in his voice edged with the anticipation of controversy '– your witnesses could all be lying, couldn't they?'

The talking around the table dwindled, and all the heads turned in Purcell's direction. Perversely, he ignored the attention he'd garnered, and turned to whisper in the ear of the boy he'd brought – a new passion who would, on past form, be discarded in a matter of weeks for another pretty urchin.

'Lying?' Helen said. She could feel herself bristling at the observation already, and Purcell had only spoken a dozen words.

'Why not?' the other replied, lifting his glass of wine to his lips. 'Perhaps they're all weaving some elaborate fiction or other. The story of the spastic's mutilation in the public toilet. The murder of the old man. Even that hook. All quite familiar elements. You must be aware that there's something *traditional* about these atrocity stories. One used to exchange them all the time; there was a certain *frisson* in them. Something competitive maybe, in attempting to find a new detail to add to the collective fiction; a fresh twist that would render the tale that little bit more appalling when you passed it on.'

'It may be familiar to you – ' said Helen, defensively. Purcell was always so *poised*; it irritated her. Even if there were validity in his argument – which she doubted – she was damned if she'd concede it. ' – *I've* never heard this kind of story before.'

'Have you not?' said Purcell, as though she were admitting to illiteracy. 'What about the lovers and the escaped lunatic, have you heard that one?'

'I've heard that…' Daniel said.

'The lover is disembowelled – usually by a hook-handed man – and the body left on the top of the car, while the fiancé cowers inside. It's a cautionary tale, warning of the evils of rampant heterosexuality.' The joke won a round of laughter from everyone but Helen. 'These stories are very common.'

'So you're saying that they're telling me lies –' she protested.

'Not lies, exactly –'

'You said *lies*.'

'I was being provocative,' Purcell returned, his placatory tone more enraging than ever. 'I don't mean to imply there's any serious mischief in it. But you *must* concede that so far you haven't met a single *witness*. All these events have happened at some unspecified date to some unspecified person. They are reported at several removes. They occurred at best to the brothers of friends of distant relations. Please consider the possibility that perhaps these events do not exist in the real world at all, but are merely titillation for bored housewives –'

Helen didn't make an argument in return, for the simple reason that she lacked one. Purcell's point about the conspicuous absence of witnesses was perfectly sound; she herself had wondered about it. It was strange, too, the way the women in Ruskin Court had speedily consigned the old man's murder to another estate, as though these atrocities always occurred just out of sight – round the next corner, down the next passageway – but never *here*.

'So why?' said Bernadette.

'Why what?' Archie puzzled.

'The stories. Why tell these horrible stories if they're not true?'

'Yes,' said Helen, throwing the controversy back into Purcell's ample lap. '*Why?*'

Purcell preened himself, aware that his entry into the debate had changed the basic assumption at a stroke. 'I don't know,' he said, happy to be done with the game now that he'd shown his arm. 'You really mustn't take me too seriously, Helen. *I* try not to.' The boy at Purcell's side tittered.

'Maybe it's simply taboo material,' Archie said.

'Suppressed −' Daniel prompted.

'Not the way you mean it,' Archie retorted. 'The whole world isn't politics, Daniel.'

'Such naiveté.'

'What's so *taboo* about death?' Trevor said. 'Bernadette already pointed out: it's in front of us all the time. Television; newspapers.'

'Maybe that's not close enough,' Bernadette suggested.

'Does anyone mind if I smoke?' Purcell broke in. 'Only dessert seems to have been indefinitely postponed −'

Helen ignored the remark, and asked Bernadette what she meant by 'not close enough'?

Bernadette shrugged. 'I don't know precisely,' she confessed, 'maybe just that death has to be *near*; we have to *know* it's just round the corner. The television's not intimate enough −'

Helen frowned. The observation made some sense to her, but in the clutter of the moment she couldn't root out its significance.

'Do you think they're stories too?' she asked.

'Andrew has a point −' Bernadette replied.

'Most kind,' said Purcell. 'Has somebody got a match? The boy's pawned my lighter.'

'− about the absence of witnesses.'

'All that proves is that I haven't met anybody who's actually *seen* anything,' Helen countered, 'not that witnesses don't exist.'

'All right,' said Purcell. 'Find me one. If you can prove to me that your atrocity-monger actually lives and breathes, I'll stand everyone dinner at Appollinaires. How's that? Am I generous to a fault, or do I just know when I can't lose?' He laughed, knocking on the table with his knuckles by way of applause.

'Sounds good to me,' said Trevor. 'What do you say, Helen?'

She didn't go back to Spector Street until the following Monday, but all weekend she was there in thought: standing outside the locked toilet, with the wind bringing rain; or in the bedroom, the portrait looming. Thoughts of the estate claimed all her concern. When, late on Saturday afternoon, Trevor found some petty reason for an argument, she let the insults pass, watching him perform the familiar ritual of self-martyrdom without being touched by it in the least. Her indifference only enraged him further. He stormed out in high dudgeon, to visit whichever of his women was in favour this month. She was glad to see the back of him. When he failed to return that night she didn't even think of weeping about it. He was foolish and vacuous. She despaired of ever seeing a haunted look in his dull eyes; and what worth was a man who could not be haunted?

He did not return Sunday night either, and it crossed her mind the following morning, as she parked her car in the heart of the estate, that nobody even knew she had come, and that she might lose herself for days here and nobody be any the wiser. Like the old man Anne-Marie had told her about: lying forgotten in his favourite armchair with his eyes hooked out, while the flies feasted and the butter went rancid on the table.

It was almost Bonfire Night, and over the weekend the

small heap of combustibles in Butts' Court had grown to a substantial size. The construction looked unsound, but that didn't prevent a number of boys and young adolescents clambering over it and into it. Much of its bulk was made up of furniture, filched, no doubt, from boarded up properties. She doubted if it could burn for any time: if it did, it would go chokingly. Four times, on her way across to Anne-Marie's house, she was waylaid by children begging for money to buy fireworks.

'Penny for the guy,' they'd say, though none had a guy to display. She had emptied her pockets of change by the time she reached the front door.

Anne-Marie was in today, though there was no welcoming smile. She simply stared at her visitor as if mesmerised.

'I hope you don't mind me calling...'

Anne-Marie made no reply.

'... I just wanted a word.'

'I'm busy,' the woman finally announced. There was no invitation inside, no offer of tea.

'Oh. Well... it won't take more than a moment.'

The back door was open and the draught blew through the house. Papers were flying about in the back yard. Helen could see them lifting into the air like vast white moths.

'What do you want?' Anne-Marie asked.

'Just to see you about the old man.'

The woman frowned minutely. She looked as if she was sickening, Helen thought: her face had the colour and texture of stale dough, her hair was lank and greasy.

'What old man?'

'Last time I was here, you told me about an old man who'd been murdered, do you remember?'

'No.'

'You said he lived in the next court.'

'I don't remember,' Anne-Marie said.

'But you *distinctly* told me –'

Something fell to the floor in the kitchen, and smashed. Anne-Marie flinched, but did not move from the doorstep, her arm barring Helen's way into the house. The hallway was littered with the child's toys, gnawed and battered.

'Are you all right?'

Anne-Marie nodded. 'I've got work to do,' she said.

'And you don't remember telling me about the old man?'

'You must have misunderstood.' Anne-Marie replied, and then, her voice hushed: 'You shouldn't have come. Everybody *knows*.'

'Knows what?'

The girl had begun to tremble. 'You don't understand, do you? You think people aren't watching?'

'What does it matter? All I asked was –'

'I don't know *anything*,' Anne-Marie reiterated. 'Whatever I said to you, I lied about it.'

'Well, thank you anyway,' Helen said, too perplexed by the confusion of signals from Anne-Marie to press the point any further. Almost as soon as she had turned from the door she heard the lock snap closed behind her.

That conversation was only one of several disappointments that morning brought. She went back to the row of shops, and visited the supermarket that Josie had spoken of. There she inquired about the lavatories, and their recent history. The supermarket had only changed hands in the last month, and the new owner, a taciturn Pakistani, insisted that he knew nothing of when or why the lavatories had been closed. She was aware, as she made her enquiries, of being scrutinized by the other customers in the shop; she felt like a pariah. That feeling deepened when, after leaving the supermarket, she saw Josie emerging from the launderette, and called after her only to have the woman pick up her pace and duck away into the maze of corridors. Helen followed, but rapidly lost both her quarry and her way.

Frustrated to the verge of tears, she stood amongst the overturned rubbish bags, and felt a surge of contempt for her foolishness. She didn't belong here, did she? How many times had she criticized others for their presumption in claiming to understand societies they had merely viewed from afar? And here she was, committing the same crime, coming here with her camera and her questions, using the lives (and deaths) of these people as fodder for party conversation. She didn't blame Anne-Marie for turning her back; had she deserved better?

Tired and chilled, she decided it was time to concede Purcell's point. It *was* all fiction she had been told. They had played with her – sensing her desire to be fed some horrors – and she, the perfect fool, had fallen for every ridiculous word. It was time to pack up her credulity and go home.

One call demanded to be made before she returned to the car however: she wanted to look a final time at the painted head. Not as an anthropologist amongst an alien tribe, but as a confessed ghost train rider: for the thrill of it. Arriving at number 14, however, she faced the last and most crushing disappointment. The maisonette had been sealed up by conscientious council workmen. The door was locked; the front window boarded over.

She was determined not to be so easily defeated however. She made her way around the back of Butts' Court and located the yard of number 14 by simple mathematics. The gate was wedged closed from the inside, but she pushed hard upon it, and, with effort on both parts, it opened. A heap of rubbish – rotted carpets, a box of rain-sodden magazines, a denuded Christmas tree – had blocked it.

She crossed the yard to the boarded up windows, and peered through the slats of wood. It wasn't bright outside, but it was darker still within; it was difficult to catch more than the vaguest hint of the painting on the bedroom wall. She pressed her face close to the wood, eager for a final glimpse.

A shadow moved across the room, momentarily blocking her view. She stepped back from the window, startled, not certain of what she'd seen. Perhaps merely her own shadow, cast through the window? But then *she* hadn't moved; it had.

She approached the window again, more cautiously. The air vibrated; she could hear a muted whine from somewhere, though she couldn't be certain whether it came from inside or out. Again, she put her face to the rough boards, and suddenly, something leapt at the window. This time she let out a cry. There was a scrabbling sound from within, as nails raked the wood.

A dog!; and a big one to have jumped so high.

'Stupid,' she told herself aloud. A sudden sweat bathed her.

The scrabbling had stopped almost as soon as it had started, but she couldn't bring herself to go back to the window. Clearly the workmen who had sealed up the maisonette had failed to check it properly, and incarcerated the animal by mistake. It was ravenous, to judge by the slavering she'd heard; she was grateful she hadn't attempted to break in. The dog – hungry, maybe half-mad in the stinking darkness – could have taken out her throat.

She stared at the boarded-up window. The slits between the boards were barely a half-inch wide, but she sensed that the animal was up on its hind legs on the other side, watching through the gap. She could hear its panting now that her own breath was regularizing; she could hear its claws raking the sill.

'Bloody thing…' she said. 'Damn well stay in there.'

She backed off towards the gate. Hosts of wood-lice and spiders, disturbed from their nests by her moving the carpets behind the gate, were scurrying underfoot, looking for a fresh darkness to call home.

She closed the gate behind her, and was making her way around the front of the block when she heard the sirens;

two ugly spirals of sound that made the hair on the back of her neck tingle. They were approaching. She picked up her speed, and came round into Butts' Court in time to see several policemen crossing the grass behind the bonfire and an ambulance mounting the pavement and driving around to the other side of the quadrangle. People had emerged from their flats and were standing on their balconies, staring down. Others were walking around the court, nakedly curious, to join a gathering congregation. Helen's stomach seemed to drop to her bowels when she realized *where* the hub of interest lay: at Anne-Marie's doorstep. The police were clearing a path through the throng for the ambulance men. A second police-car had followed the route of the ambulance onto the pavement; two plain-clothes officers were getting out.

She walked to the periphery of the crowd. What little talk there was amongst the on-lookers was conducted in low voices; one or two of the older women were crying. Though she peered over the heads of the spectators she could see nothing. Turning to a bearded man, whose child was perched on his shoulders, she asked what was going on. He didn't know. Somebody dead, he'd heard, but he wasn't certain.

'Anne-Marie?' she asked.

A woman in front of her turned and said: 'You know her?' almost awed, as if speaking of a loved one.

'A little,' Helen replied hesitantly. 'Can you tell me what's happened?'

The woman involuntarily put her hand to her mouth, as if to stop the words before they came. But here they were nevertheless: 'The child – ' she said.

'Kerry?'

'Somebody got into the house around the back. Slit his throat.'

Helen felt the sweat come again. In her mind's eye the newspapers rose and fell in Anne-Marie's yard.

74

'No,' she said.

'Just like that.'

She looked at the tragedian who was trying to sell her this obscenity, and said, 'No,' again. It defied belief; yet her denials could not silence the horrid comprehension she felt.

She turned her back on the woman and paddled her way out of the crowd. There was nothing to see, she knew, and even if there had been she had no desire to look. These people – still emerging from their homes as the story spread – were exhibiting an appetite she was disgusted by. She was not one of them; would never *be* of them. She wanted to slap every eager face into sense; wanted to say: 'It's pain and grief you're going to spy on. Why? Why?' But she had no courage left. Revulsion had drained her of all but the energy to wander away, leaving the crowd to its sport.

Trevor had come home. He did not attempt an explanation of his absence, but waited for her to cross-question him. When she failed to do so he sank into an easy *bonhomie* that was worse than his expectant silence. She was dimly aware that her disinterest was probably more unsettling for him than the histrionics he had been anticipating. She couldn't have cared less.

She tuned the radio to the local station, and listened for news. It came surely enough, confirming what the woman in the crowd had told her. Kerry Latimer was dead. Person or persons unknown had gained access to the house via the back yard and murdered the child while he played on the kitchen floor. A police spokesman mouthed the usual platitudes, describing Kerry's death as an 'unspeakable crime', and the miscreant as 'a dangerous and deeply disturbed individual'. For once, the rhetoric seemed justified, and the man's voice shook discernibly when he spoke of the scene that had confronted the officers in the kitchen of Anne-Marie's house.

'Why the radio?' Trevor casually inquired, when Helen

listened for news through three consecutive bulletins. She saw no point in withholding her experience at Spector Street from him; he would find out sooner or later. Coolly, she gave him a bald outline of what had happened at Butts' Court.

'This Anne-Marie is the woman you met when you first went to the estate; am I right?'

She nodded, hoping he wouldn't ask her too many questions. Tears were close, and she had no intention of breaking down in front of him.

'So you were right,' he said.

'Right?'

'About the place having a maniac.'

'No,' she said. 'No.'

'But the kid —'

She got up and stood at the window, looking down two storeys into the darkened street below. Why did she feel the need to reject the conspiracy theory so urgently?; why was she now praying that Purcell had been right, and that all she'd been told had been lies? She went back and back to the way Anne-Marie had been when she'd visited her that morning: pale, jittery; *expectant*. She had been like a woman anticipating some arrival, hadn't she?, eager to shoo unwanted visitors away so that she could turn back to the business of waiting. But waiting for what, or *whom*? Was it possible that Anne-Marie actually knew the murderer? Had perhaps invited him into the house?

'I hope they find the bastard,' she said, still watching the street.

'They will,' Trevor replied. 'A baby-murderer, for Christ's sake. They'll make that a high priority.'

A man appeared at the corner of the street, turned, and whistled. A large Alsatian came to heel, and the two set off down towards the Cathedral.

'The dog,' Helen murmured.

'What?'

She had forgotten the dog in all that had followed. Now the shock she'd felt as it had leapt at the window shook her again.

'What dog?' Trevor pressed.

'I went back to the flat today – where I took the pictures of the graffiti. There was a dog in there. Locked in.'

'So?'

'It'll starve. Nobody knows it's there.'

'How do you know it wasn't locked in to kennel it?'

'It was making such a noise –' she said.

'Dogs bark,' Trevor replied. 'That's all they're good for.'

'No...' she said very quietly, remembering the noises through the boarded window. 'It didn't bark... '

'Forget the dog,' Trevor said. 'And the child. There's nothing you can do about it. You were just passing through.'

His words only echoed her own thoughts of earlier in the day, but somehow – for reasons that she could find no words to convey – that conviction had decayed in the last hours. She was not just passing through. Nobody ever just *passed through*; experience always left its mark. Sometimes, it merely scratched; on occasion it took off limbs. She did not know the extent of her present wounding, but she knew it more profound than she yet understood, and it made her afraid.

'We're out of booze,' she said, emptying the last dribble of whisky into her tumbler.

Trevor seemed pleased to have a reason to be accommodating. 'I'll go out, shall I?' he said. 'Get a bottle or two?'

'Sure,' she replied. 'If you like.'

He was gone only half an hour; she would have liked him to have been longer. She didn't want to talk, only sit and think through the unease in her belly. Though Trevor had dismissed her concern for the dog – and perhaps justifiably so – she couldn't help but go back to the locked maisonette in her mind's eye: to picture again the raging face on the bedroom wall, and hear the animal's muffled growl as it pawed the boards over the window. Whatever Trevor had said, she didn't believe the place was being used as a makeshift kennel. No, the dog was *imprisoned* in there, no doubt of it, running round and round, driven, in its desperation, to eat its own faeces, growing more insane with every hour that passed. She became afraid that somebody – kids maybe, looking for more tinder for their bonfire – would break into the place, ignorant of what it contained. It wasn't that she feared for the intruders' safety, but that the dog, once liberated, would come for her. It would know where she was (so her drunken head construed) and come sniffing her out.

Trevor returned with the whisky, and they drank together until the early hours, when her stomach revolted. She took refuge in the toilet – Trevor outside asking her if she needed anything, her telling him weakly to leave her alone. When, an hour later, she emerged, he had gone to bed. She did not join him, but lay down on the sofa and dozed through until dawn.

The murder was news. The next morning it made all the tabloids as a front page splash, and found prominent positions in the heavy-weights too. There were photographs of the stricken mother being led from the house, and others, blurred but potent, taken over the back yard wall and through the open kitchen door. Was that blood on the floor, or shadow?

Helen did not bother to read the articles – her aching head rebelled at the thought – but Trevor, who had brought the newspapers in, was eager to talk. She couldn't work out if this was further peacemaking on his part, or a genuine interest in the issue.

'The woman's in custody,' he said, poring over the *Daily Telegraph*. It was a paper he was politically averse to, but its coverage of violent crime was notoriously detailed.

The observation demanded Helen's attention, unwilling or not. 'Custody?' she said. 'Anne-Marie?'

'Yes.'

'Let me see.'

He relinquished the paper, and she glanced over the page.

'Third column,' Trevor prompted.

She found the place, and there it was in black and white. Anne-Marie had been taken into custody for questioning to justify the time-lapse between the estimated hour of the child's death, and the time that it had been reported. Helen read the relevant sentences over again, to be certain that she'd understood properly. Yes, she had. The police pathologist estimated Kerry to have died between six and six-thirty that morning; the murder had not been reported until twelve.

She read the report over a third and a fourth time, but repetition did not change the horrid facts. The child had been murdered before dawn. When she had gone to the house that morning Kerry had already been dead four hours. The body had been in the kitchen, a few yards down the hallway from where she had stood, and Anne-Marie had said *nothing*. That air of expectancy she had had about her – what had it signified? That she awaited some cue to lift the receiver and call the police?

'My Christ... ' Helen said, and let the paper drop.

'What?'

'I have to go to the police.'

'Why?'

'To tell them I went to the house,' she replied. Trevor looked mystified. 'The baby was dead, Trevor. When I saw Anne-Marie yesterday morning, Kerry was already dead.'

She rang the number given in the paper for any persons offering information, and half an hour later a police car came to pick her up. There was much that startled her in the two hours of interrogation that followed, not least that nobody had reported her presence on the estate to the police, though she had surely been noticed.

'They don't want to know –' the detective told her, '– you'd think a place like that would be swarming with witnesses. If it is, they're not coming forward. A crime like this... '

'Is it the first?'

He looked at her across a chaotic desk. 'First?'

'I was told some stories about the estate. Murders. This summer.'

The detective shook his head. 'Not to my knowledge. There's been a spate of muggings; one woman was put in hospital for a week or so. But no; no murders.'

She liked the detective. His eyes flattered her with their lingering, his face with their frankness. Past caring whether she sounded foolish or not, she said: 'Why do they tell lies like that. About people having their eyes cut out. Terrible things.'

The detective scratched his long nose. 'We get it too,' he said. 'People come in here, they confess to all kinds of crap. Talk all night, some of them, about things they've done, or *think* they've done. Give you it all in the minutest detail. And when you make a few calls, it's all invented. Out of their minds.'

'Maybe if they didn't tell you the stories... they'd actually go out and do it.'

The detective nodded. 'Yes,' he said. 'God help us. You might be right at that.'

And the stories *she'd* been told, were they confessions of uncommitted crimes?, accounts of the worst imaginable, imagined to keep fiction from becoming fact? The thought chased its own tail: these terrible stories still needed a *first cause*, a well-spring from which they leapt. As she walked home through the busy streets she wondered how many of her fellow citizens knew such stories. Were these inventions common currency, as Purcell had claimed? Was there a place, however small, reserved in every heart for the monstrous?

'Purcell rang,' Trevor told her when she got home. 'To invite us out to dinner.'

The invitation wasn't welcome, and she made a face.

'Appollinaires, remember?' he reminded her. 'He said he'd take us all to dinner, if you proved him wrong.'

The thought of getting a dinner out of the death of Anne-Marie's infant was grotesque, and she said so.

'He'll be offended if you turn him down.'

'I don't give a damn. I don't want dinner with Purcell.'

'Please,' he said softly. 'He can get difficult; and I want to keep him smiling just a moment.'

She glanced across at him. The look he'd put on made him resemble a drenched spaniel. Manipulative bastard, she thought; but said: 'All right, I'll go. But don't expect any dancing on the tables.'

'We'll leave that to Archie,' he said. 'I told Purcell we were free tomorrow night. Is that all right with you?'

'Whenever.'

'He's booking a table for eight o'clock.'

The evening papers had relegated The Tragedy of Baby Kerry to a few column inches on an inside page. In lieu of much fresh news they simply described the house-to-house enquiries that were now going on at Spector Street. Some of the later editions mentioned that Anne-Marie had been released from custody after an extended period of questioning, and was now residing with friends. They also mentioned, in passing, that the funeral was to be the following day.

Helen had not entertained any thoughts of going back to Spector Street for the funeral when she went to bed that night, but sleep seemed to change her mind, and she woke with the decision made for her.

Death had brought the estate to life. Walking through to Ruskin Court from the street she had never seen such numbers out and about. Many were already lining the kerb to watch the funeral cortège pass, and looked to have claimed their niche early, despite the wind and the ever-present threat of rain. Some were wearing items of black clothing – a coat, a scarf – but the overall impression, despite the lowered voices and the studied frowns, was one of celebration. Children running around, untouched by reverence; occasional laughter escaping from between gossiping adults – Helen could feel an air of anticipation which made her spirits, despite the occasion, almost buoyant.

Nor was it simply the presence of so many people that reassured her; she was, she conceded to herself, happy to be back here in Spector Street. The quadrangles, with their stunted saplings and their grey grass, were more real to her than the carpeted corridors she was used to walking; the anonymous faces on the balconies and streets meant more than her colleagues at the University. In a word, she felt *home*.

Finally, the cars appeared, moving at a snail's pace through the narrow streets. As the hearse came into view – its tiny white casket decked with flowers – a number of women in the crowd gave quiet voice to their grief. One on-looker fainted; a knot of anxious people gathered around her. Even the children were stilled now.

Helen watched, dry-eyed. Tears did not come very easily to her, especially in company. As the second car, containing Anne-Marie and two other women, drew level with her, Helen saw that the bereaved mother was also eschewing any public display of grief. She seemed, indeed, to be almost elevated by the proceedings, sitting upright in the back of the car, her pallid features the source of much admiration. It was a sour thought, but Helen felt as though she was seeing Anne-Marie's finest hour; the one day in an otherwise anonymous life in which she was the centre of attention. Slowly, the cortège passed by and disappeared from view.

The crowd around Helen was already dispersing. She detached herself from the few mourners who still lingered at the kerb and wandered through from the street into Butts' Court. It was her intention to go back to the locked maisonette, to see if the dog was still there. If it was, she would put her mind to rest by finding one of the estate caretakers and informing him of the fact.

The quadrangle was, unlike the other courts, practically empty. Perhaps the residents, being neighbours of Anne-Marie's, had gone on to the Crematorium for the service. Whatever the reason, the place was eerily deserted. Only children remained, playing around the pyramid bonfire, their voices echoing across the empty expanse of the square.

She reached the maisonette and was surprised to find the door open again, as it had been the first time she'd come here. The sight of the interior made her light-headed. How often in the past several days had she imagined standing here, gazing into that darkness. There was no sound from inside. The dog had surely run off; either that, or died. There could be no harm, could there?, in stepping into the place one final time, just to look at the face on the wall, and its attendant slogan.

Sweets to the sweet. She had never looked up the origins of that phrase. No matter, she thought. Whatever it had stood for once, it was transformed here, as everything was; herself included. She stood in the front room for a few moments, to allow herself time to savour the confrontation ahead. Far away behind her the children were screeching like mad birds.

She stepped over a clutter of furniture and towards the short corridor that joined living-room to bedroom, still delaying the moment. Her heart was quick in her: a smile played on her lips.

83

And there! At last! The portrait loomed, compelling as ever. She stepped back in the murky room to admire it more fully and her heel caught on the mattress that still lay in the corner. She glanced down. The squalid bedding had been turned over, to present its untorn face. Some blankets and a rag-wrapped pillow had been tossed over it. Something glistened amongst the folds of the uppermost blanket. She bent down to look more closely and found there a handful of sweets – chocolates and caramels – wrapped in bright paper. And littered amongst them, neither so attractive nor so sweet, a dozen razor-blades. There was blood on several. She stood up again and backed away from the mattress, and as she did so a buzzing sound reached her ears from the next room. She turned, and the light in the bedroom diminished as a figure stepped into the gullet between her and the outside world. Silhouetted against the light, she could scarcely see the man in the doorway, but she smelt him. He smelt like candy-floss; and the buzzing was with him or in him.

'I just came to look –' she said, '– at the picture.'

The buzzing went on: the sound of a sleepy afternoon, far from here. The man in the doorway did not move.

'Well...' she said, 'I've seen what I wanted to see.' She hoped against hope that her words would prompt him to stand aside and let her past, but he didn't move, and she couldn't find the courage to challenge him by stepping towards the door.

'I have to go,' she said, knowing that despite her best efforts fear seeped between every syllable. 'I'm expected... '
That was not entirely untrue. Tonight they were all invited to Appollinaires for dinner. But that wasn't till eight, which was four hours away. She would not be missed for a long while yet.

'If you'll excuse me,' she said.

The buzzing had quietened a little, and in the hush the man in the doorway spoke. His unaccented voice was almost as sweet as his scent.

'No need to leave yet,' he breathed.

'I'm due... due...'

Though she couldn't see his eyes, she felt them on her, and they made her feel drowsy, like that summer that sang in her head.

'I came for you,' he said.

She repeated the four words in her head. *I came for you* If they were meant as a threat, they certainly weren't spoken as one.

'I don't... know you,' she said.

'No,' the man murmured. 'But you doubted me.'

'Doubted?'

'You weren't content with the stories, with what they wrote on the walls. So I was obliged to come.'

The drowsiness slowed her mind to a crawl, but she grasped the essentials of what the man was saying. That he was legend, and she, in disbelieving in him, had obliged him to show his hand. She looked, now, down at those hands. One of them was missing. In its place, a hook.

'There will be some blame,' he told her. 'They will say your doubts shed innocent blood. But I say – what's blood for, if not for shedding? And in time the scrutiny will pass. The police will leave, the cameras will be pointed at some fresh horror, and they will be left alone, to tell stories of the Candyman again.'

'Candyman?' she said. Her tongue could barely shape that blameless word.

'I came for you,' he murmured so softly that seduction might have been in the air. And so saying, he moved through the passageway and into the light.

She knew him, without doubt. She had known him all along, in that place kept for terrors. It was the man on the wall. His portrait painter had not been a fantasist: the picture that howled over her was matched in each extraordinary particular by the man she now set eyes upon. He was bright to the point of gaudiness: his flesh a waxy yellow, his thin lips pale blue, his wild eyes glittering as if their irises were set with rubies. His jacket was a patchwork, his trousers the same. He looked, she thought, almost ridiculous, with his blood-stained motley, and the hint of rouge on his jaundiced cheeks. But people were facile. They needed these shows and shams to keep their interest. Miracles; murders; demons driven out and stones rolled from tombs. The cheap glamour did not taint the sense beneath. It was only, in the natural history of the mind, the bright feathers that drew the species to mate with its secret self.

And she was almost enchanted. By his voice, by his colours, by the buzz from his body. She fought to resist the rapture, though. There was a *monster* here, beneath this fetching display; its nest of razors was at her feet, still drenched in blood. Would it hesitate to slit her own throat if it once laid hands on her?

As the Candyman reached for her she dropped down and snatched the blanket up, flinging it at him. A rain of razors and sweetmeats fell around his shoulders. The blanket followed, blinding him, the pillow which had lain on the blanket rolled in front of her.

It was not a pillow at all. Whatever the forlorn white casket she had seen in the hearse had contained, it was not the body of Baby Kerry. That was *here*, at her feet, its blood-drained face turned up to her. He was naked. His body showed everywhere signs of the fiend's attentions.

In the two heartbeats she took to register this last horror, the Candyman threw off the blanket. In his struggle to escape from its folds, his jacket had come unbuttoned, and she saw – though her sense protested – that the contents of his torso had rotted away, and the hollow was now occupied by a nest of bees. They swarmed in the vault of his chest, and encrusted in a seething mass the remnants of flesh that hung there. He smiled at her plain repugnance.

'Sweets to the sweet,' he murmured, and stretched his hooked hand towards her face. She could no longer see light from the outside world, nor hear the children playing in Butts' Court. There was no escape into a saner world than this. The Candyman filled her sight; her drained limbs had no strength to hold him at bay.

'Don't kill me,' she breathed.

'Do you believe in me?' he said.

She nodded minutely. 'How can I not?' she said.

'Then why do you want to live?'

She didn't understand, and was afraid her ignorance would prove fatal, so she said nothing.

'If you would learn,' the fiend said, 'just a *little* from me... you would not beg to live.' His voice had dropped to a whisper. 'I am rumour,' he sang in her ear. 'It's blessed condition, believe me. To live in people's dreams; to be whispered at street-corners; but not have to *be*. Do you understand?'

Her weary body understood. Her nerves, tired of jangling, understood. The sweetness he offered was life without living: was to be dead, but remembered everywhere; immortal in gossip and graffiti.

'Be my victim,' he said.

'No... ' she murmured.

'I won't force it upon you,' he replied, the perfect gentleman. 'I won't oblige you to die. But think; *think*. If I kill you here – if I unhook you...' he traced the path of the promised wound with his hook. It ran from groin to neck. 'Think how they would mark this place with their talk... point it out as they passed by and say: '*She* died there; the woman with the green eyes'. Your death would be a parable to frighten children with. Lovers would use it as an excuse to cling closer together...'

She had been right: this *was* a seduction.

'Was fame ever so easy?' he asked.

She shook her head. 'I'd prefer to be forgotten,' she replied, 'than remembered like that.'

He made a tiny shrug. 'What do the good know?' he

said. 'Except what the bad teach them by their excesses?' He raised his hooked hand. 'I said I would not oblige you to die and I'm true to my word. Allow me, though, a kiss at least...'

He moved towards her. She murmured some nonsensical threat, which he ignored. The buzzing in his body had risen in volume. The thought of touching his body, of the proximity of the insects, was horrid. She forced her lead-heavy arms up to keep him at bay.

His lurid face eclipsed the portrait on the wall. She couldn't bring herself to touch him, and instead stepped back. The sound of the bees rose; some, in their excitement, had crawled up his throat and were flying from his mouth. They climbed about his lips; in his hair.

She begged him over and over to leave her alone, but he would not be placated. At last she had nowhere left to retreat to; the wall was at her back. Steeling herself against the stings, she put her hand on his crawling chest and pushed. As she did so his hand shot out and around the back of her neck, the hook nicking the flushed skin of her throat. She felt blood come; felt certain he would open her jugular in one terrible slash. But he had given his word: and he was true to it.

Aroused by this sudden activity, the bees were everywhere. She felt them moving on her, searching for morsels of wax in her ears, and sugar at her lips. She made no attempt to swat them away. The hook was at her neck. If she so much as moved it would wound her. She was trapped, as in her childhood nightmares, with every chance of escape stymied. When sleep had brought her to such hopelessness – the demons on every side, waiting to tear her limb from limb – one trick remained. To let go; to give up all ambition to life, and leave her body in the dark. Now, as the Candyman's face pressed to hers, and the sounds of bees blotted out even her own breath, she played that hidden hand. And, as surely as in dreams, the room and the fiend were painted out and gone.

She woke from brightness into dark. There were several panicked moments when she couldn't think of where she was, then several more when she remembered. But there was no pain about her body. She put her hand to her neck; it was, barring the nick of the hook, untouched. She was lying on the mattress she realized. Had she been assaulted as she lay faint? Gingerly, she investigated her body. She was not bleeding; her clothes were not disturbed. The Candyman had, it seemed, simply claimed his kiss.

She sat up. There was precious little light through the boarded window – and none from the front door. Perhaps it was closed, she reasoned. But no; even now she heard somebody whispering on the threshold. A woman's voice.

She didn't move. They were crazy, these people. They had known all along what her presence in Butts' Court had summoned, and they had *protected* him – this honeyed psychopath; given him a bed and an offering of bonbons, hidden away from prying eyes, and kept their silence when he brought blood to their doorsteps. Even Anne-Marie, dry-eyed in the hallway of her house, knowing that her child was dead a few yards away.

The child! That was the evidence she needed. Somehow they had conspired to get the body from the casket (what had they substituted; the dead dog?) and brought it here – to the Candyman's tabernacle – as a toy, or a lover. She would take Baby Kerry with her – to the police – and tell the whole story. Whatever they believed of it – and that would probably be very little – the fact of the child's body was incontestable. That way at least some of the crazies would suffer for their conspiracy. Suffer for *her* suffering.

The whispering at the door had stopped. Now somebody was moving towards the bedroom. They didn't bring a light with them. Helen made herself small, hoping she might escape detection.

A figure appeared in the doorway. The gloom was too

impenetrable for her to make out more than a slim figure, who bent down and picked up a bundle on the floor. A fall of blond hair identified the newcomer as Anne-Marie: the bundle she was picking up was undoubtedly Kerry's corpse. Without looking in Helen's direction, the mother about-turned and made her way out of the bedroom.

Helen listened as the footsteps receded across the living-room. Swiftly, she got to her feet, and crossed to the passageway. From there she could vaguely see Anne-Marie's outline in the doorway of the maisonette. No lights burned in the quadrangle beyond. The woman disappeared and Helen followed as speedily as she could, eyes fixed on the door ahead. She stumbled once, and once again, but reached the door in time to see Anne-Marie's vague form in the night ahead.

She stepped out of the maisonette and into the open air. It was chilly; there were no stars. All the lights on the balconies and corridors were out, nor did any burn in the flats; not even the glow of a television. Butts' Court was deserted.

She hesitated before going in pursuit of the girl. Why didn't she slip away now?, cowardice coaxed her, and find her way back to the car? But if she did that the conspirators would have time to conceal the child's body. When she got back here with the police there would be sealed lips and shrugs, and she would be told she had imagined the corpse and the Candyman. All the terrors she had tasted would recede into rumour again. Into words on a wall. And every day she lived from now on she would loathe herself for not going in pursuit of sanity.

She followed. Anne-Marie was not making her way around the quadrangle, but moving towards the centre of the lawn in the middle of the court. To the bonfire! Yes; to the bonfire! It loomed in front of Helen now, blacker than the night-sky. She could just make out Anne-Marie's figure, moving to the edge of the piled timbers and furniture, and ducking to climb into its heart. *This* was how they planned to remove the evidence. To bury the child was not certain enough; but to cremate it, and pound the bones – who would ever know?

She stood a dozen yards from the pyramid and watched as Anne-Marie climbed out again and moved away, folding her figure into the darkness.

Quickly, Helen moved through the long grass and located the narrow space in amongst the piled timbers into which Anne-Marie had put the body. She thought she could see the pale form; it had been laid in a hollow. She couldn't reach it however. Thanking God that she was as slim as the mother, she squeezed through the narrow aperture. Her dress snagged on a nail as she did so. She turned around to disengage it, fingers trembling. When she turned back she had lost sight of the corpse.

She fumbled blindly ahead of her, her hands finding wood and rags and what felt like the back of an old armchair, but not the cold skin of the child. She had hardened herself against contact with the body: she had endured worse in the last hours than picking up a dead baby. Determined not to be defeated, she advanced a little further, her shins scraped and her fingers spiked with splinters. Flashes of light were appearing at the corners of her aching eyes; her blood whined in her ears. But there!; *there*!; the body was no more than a yard and a half ahead of her. She ducked down to reach beneath a beam of wood, but her fingers missed the forlorn bundle by millimetres. She stretched further, the whine in her head increasing, but still she could not reach the child. All she could do was bend double and squeeze into the hidey-hole the children had left at the centre of the bonfire.

It was difficult to get through. The space was so small she could barely crawl on hands and knees; but she made it. The child lay face down. She fought back the remnants of squeamishness and went to pick it up. As she did so, something landed on her arm. The shock startled her. She almost cried out, but swallowed the urge, and brushed the irritation away. It buzzed as it rose from her skin. The whine she had heard in her ears was not her blood, but the hive.

'I knew you'd come,' the voice behind her said, and a wide hand covered her face. She fell backwards and the Candyman embraced her.

'We have to go,' he said in her ear, as flickering light spilled between the stacked timbers. 'Be on our way, you and I.'

She fought to be free of him, to cry out for them not to light the bonfire, but he held her lovingly close. The light grew: warmth came with it; and through the kindling and the first flames she could see figures approaching the pyre out of the darkness of Butts' Court. They had been there all along: waiting, the lights turned out in their homes, and broken all along the corridors. Their final conspiracy.

The bonfire caught with a will, but by some trick of its construction the flames did not invade her hiding-place quickly; nor did the smoke creep through the furniture to choke her. She was able to watch how the children's faces gleamed; how the parents called them from going too close, and how they disobeyed; how the old women, their blood thin, warmed their hands and smiled into the flames. Presently the roar and the crackle became deafening, and the Candyman let her scream herself hoarse in the certain knowledge that nobody could hear her, and even if they had would not have moved to claim her from the fire.

The bees vacated the fiend's belly as the air became hotter, and mazed the air with their panicked flight. Some, attempting escape, caught fire, and fell like tiny meteors to the ground. The body of Baby Kerry, which lay close to the creeping flames, began to cook. Its downy hair smoked, its back blistered.

Soon the heat crept down Helen's throat, and scorched her pleas away. She sank back, exhausted, into the Candyman's arms, resigned to his triumph. In moments they would be on their way, as he had promised, and there was no help for it.

Perhaps they would remember her, as he had said they might, finding her cracked skull in tomorrow's ashes. Perhaps she might become, in time, a story with which to frighten children. She had lied, saying she preferred death to such questionable fame; she did not. As to her seducer, he laughed as the conflagration sniffed them out. There was to be no permanence for him in this night's death. His deeds were on a hundred walls and ten thousand lips, and should he be doubted again his congregation could summon him with sweetness. He had reason to laugh. So, as the flames crept upon them, did she, as through the fire she caught sight of a familiar face moving between the on-lookers. It was Trevor. He had forsaken his meal at Appollinaires and come looking for her.

She watched him questioning this fire-watcher and that, but they shook their heads, all the while staring at the pyre with smiles buried in their eyes. Poor dupe, she thought, following his antics. She willed him to look past the flames in the hope that he might see her burning. Not so that he could save her from death – she was long past hope of that – but because she pitied him his bewilderment and wanted to give him, though he would not have thanked her for it, something to be haunted by. That, and a story to tell.

Low Visibility

Margaret Murphy

John is watching TV, one hand on the remote control, the other on her thigh. She keeps very still.

The news is on – always a serious business, but tonight it is momentous. A car burns in the centre of the road. Thirty or forty people have gathered, most are armed, some wear masks; on the other side, the police form a nervous line behind plastic shields. The mob hold on to their stones, their bottles and half-bricks, content, for the moment, to hurl abuse.

'Scum,' John says.

A flash of something white and orange shoots high into the night, over the burning car, spiralling as it falls, a looping script of flame and smoke. The bottle smashes at the feet of the police cordon and fire leaps, a splash of heat, a puddle of flame, curling around the edges of the shields, prying at the chinks in their defences. They shuffle back a few steps and the crowd roars in triumph.

'What are they protesting about?' John demands. 'Their own shitty lives?'

She wishes *she* could protest, but has forgotten how. Every muscle in her body trembles with the effort of keeping still.

John digs his fingers into her thigh and she bites her lip, but doesn't move, and after a few seconds the pressure decreases, leaving only a dull throb.

She wasn't always like this. Once, she was a girl who could set a room to laughter. He wanted her for her spirit and energy, her exuberance. He thought that her good humour would seep into him, breaching the walls of his defences, that happiness was something that could be absorbed, as a plant takes in water, by osmosis. But he hadn't the intelligence for wit or the disposition for contentment, so he held her too tight, his hostage and his shield, squeezing the joy out of her until there was none left.

She barely noticed the change, but gradually she stopped feeling the sting of outrage, the injustice of his unkind words, his indiscriminate criticisms. By slow degrees she began to expect them, like the dripping tap he never fixed, constant, insistent, the white noise of their marriage.

The slaps and shoves that at first shocked her, became something to be expected; they reshaped her, moulding her into something less distinct, more insubstantial.

He has always been good with his hands.

'Vermin,' he says, and she feels the pressure of his fingers, testing for a tender spot, finding the bone. She winces in anticipation of the pain and he feels the movement, notices her. Turns his head and she feels his gaze on her.

'Did you say something?'

She shakes her head – just enough so he knows she didn't mean to interrupt, not so much he might think her adamant in her denial. But she can't stop her breathing, the rise and fall of her chest.

'Nothing to *contribute*?'

Her heart flutters in her chest.

'No sharp *insights* into the situation?'

She is wordless, stripped of language, of the liberty of expression. She doesn't know the right thing to say, because he changes the rules each time. So she says nothing. It's safer – less painful.

He's distracted from her by the flicker of light from the TV. For John, the cohesion of dots on the screen has substance where she has none. Another arc of flame rises over the heads of the mob, over the burning car. It smashes on the ground and sends a second wave of liquid heat at the police defences. They retreat another few steps and she feels a kind of wonder. Had these people simply tired of staying still? Perhaps they felt an ache of inertia in their bones and had to act.

She wonders how it would feel to shout, to throw things, to see John scuttle back behind his barrier of hate.

It is warm – barbecue weather. Perhaps it is the heat, or perhaps the rage of the mob satiates him, for John settles back on the sofa and for a time, forgets she is there. His hand does not forget, though: as violence leaps like sparks from a forest fire, setting up plumes of smoke across the city, he hurts her. Twists and kneads, probing, bruising her flesh. Better this, she thinks, than his fist or his elbow. Better that he hurts her absent-mindedly, as a man might puncture and tear at the rim of a polystyrene cup. It comforts her that there is no malice in it. She has learned to find solace in small things.

The television cameras switch to Upper Parliament Street. A wide stretch of road, a barrier built from a van, a burnt-out milk float, a VW Beetle, the silvery sheen of its metallic finish peeled off like plastic in the heat. The reporter sounds afraid. A baker's delivery van turns into the road, brakes hard and starts to reverse, fishtailing wildly back the way it came. But it hits a pothole and loses control, smashes into the wall of a derelict building. The mob is on him. They drag the driver from the van and beat him. His van is overturned and set alight as the fire brigade sirens wail inconsolably beyond the police line.

'Animals,' John mutters, feasting on her pain.

Lodge Lane: a steady flow of people wheel tartan shopping trolleys with flap tops, or tote bulging carrier bags, their knees sagging with the weight. It's fully dark – the wires of smashed street lamps hang like the intestines of eviscerated corpses. The TV crew interviews a woman. She is a quarter of a mile from the nearest supermarket, and her supermarket trolley is brimming with food. 'What am I *like*?' she laughs, giddy with adrenaline. 'I was pushing this thing round Kwik Save, looking for the bargains.' She snorts at her own stupidity.

The journalist is young – breathless with terror – but ambition gives him courage. 'They're looting the shops?' he says, with a sly glance to the camera. Does it ever get better than this on local TV news?

'The door was open,' she says tartly, not liking the tag of 'looter'. 'And there wasn't no one on the tills.'

'Is there *anything* left in Kwik Save?' His tone is plaintive, his expression earnest.

'I think I saw a packet of sausages on the meat counter,' she says, unleashing her sarcasm.

'No-marks,' John says. 'Selfish bastards.' John, who takes what he wants, never thinking to ask. Never thinking of her at all.

Warm air stirs the curtain, bringing the reek of burning fuel and soot. Is the whole city ablaze? The roar of the mob on TV, the howl of sirens, the excited babble of the journalists cover an insistent bass note, a murmur of voices. For now, they're in her head, but they are coming: she can feel the crackle of tension like an electrical charge in the air.

A glass smashes and she jumps.

He misunderstands its proximity, having grown used to viewing the world through the letterbox of his TV set. He slaps her with the back of his hand, his knuckles bruising her cheekbone.

'Sit still, you twitchy cow,' he says. When he replaces his hand, he moves it higher up her thigh. This is his foreplay, his substitute for romance.

She tastes blood, but dares not reach up to wipe her mouth. At such moments, she allows herself to float away, imagines she is a million particles of matter that can simply disperse: it makes what will inevitably follow endurable. This is not without risk – it takes time for the particles to find their way back to her, an effort of will to bind the essence of herself together again. She has lost some of the constituent matter over the years; the light is dimmer, the colours a little faded.

Shouts drift up from the street and he points the remote control at the TV, lowering the volume. Three solid thuds rattle chunks of plaster from the ceiling, then a cheer, and the sound of footsteps on bare boards.

They're in the shop below. He paces to the window and pulls up the sash. 'Get out of there, you robbing bastards!'

They aren't listening. She hears them crashing about, rummaging through the cheap crockery and plastic bric-a-brac. He crosses the room and flings the door open.

She stands, afraid of what he might do.

'Don't.' The sound of her voice startles her. She hasn't spoken a word of command in four years.

John stares in her direction, as if trying to locate the source of the sound, but he sees no more than a shimmer of something against the orange glow beyond the curtains. She has become invisible.

He turns and she hears the thud of his boots, feels the joists tremble under him. People say he's light on his feet for a big man, but he was never so with her. When he walked all over her, she felt it.

Her hand goes to her jeans pocket, and she takes out a tiger eye stone, a gift from a friend. 'For courage,' her friend said. It didn't cost much – John's wife is not to be trusted with anything of value. 'The tiger eye, creates harmony out of chaos,' her friend told her. 'Heals bruises, alleviates pain.' She could have hired herself out as an experimental subject on the healing properties of gemstones.

Family, friends, religion, hope, have all rushed past her, like corks lost in the torrent of his rage. She clings to this last plank of her previous existence in the blind faith that it will keep her from going under for good.

She hears shouts from below. His voice raised in anger. She trembles, staring into the tiger eye for strength. Sometimes when she gazes into its depths she sees only gathering darkness, but on rare, magical moments she sees a flash of light spark from the amber stripe at its centre and feels a stirring of something within her – spirit, perhaps, or hope.

She hears his voice in the street and creeps to the window. He is fighting. When he falls, at first she is afraid. She should have gone with him. Should have persuaded him to stay. Should somehow have stopped all of this happening. She will be blamed. She backs into the shadows, hears a rumble of noise as the looters run out of the shop, whooping. She smells burning candle wax and something more acrid. Wisps of smoke slide up the staircase, into the room. She feels heat through the soles of her feet. The shop is ablaze.

She slips her shoes on and runs, the tiger eye tight in her palm.

★

Seconds later she is in the street amid the thick blue stench of petrol fumes, charred wood and burning plastic. All down the wide stretch of road, fires rage, and a smutfall of sooty flakes spins down. A block away, they have set fire to the bakery, and incongruously, the chemical smells are overlaid with the reek of burnt toast.

John lies on his back. His head is bleeding. She looks right and left – but invisibility is not cast off lightly. Two men lug a fridge from the electrical shop and vanish down a side street; others emerge. Radios, an iron, a portable TV, are all carried off. The toy shop has a festival atmosphere: Christmas has come early, and Santa is in generous mood. An existence of want has exploded into wanting – the sensory: food, textures, flavours, colour – and the material: the shiny, the new. They carry their stolen trinkets like trophies.

She alone is silent amid the noise, still in the confusion of screams, the shriek of burning houses, the keening of the sirens. A wind rushes in from the Mersey, drawn by the heat and the hunger of the inferno. They have unleashed a firestorm that will change the landscape of their lives for ever.

John stirs and moans and she feels a stab of fear. He opens his eyes. And her heart stops. He sees her.

'Give us your hand.' He has spoken.

It occurs to her that she might not. The thought is exhilarating.

He raises himself to his elbows and a ripple of alarm tingles from the top of her head to her fingertips. 'What are you waiting for?'

She looks at his hand extended towards her, demanding help; the fingers are bloody. She doesn't want blood on her hands.

A man pushing a stolen trolley approaches. One wheel is wonky, it balks and judders, and he has to keep redirecting its course, but he does the work with jaunty good will.

John begs for help, but the man seems not to hear. 'Save a mint on the rental,' he says as he passes, dropping her a friendly wink.

She marvels that he sees her – sees *her* and not John. John has never been invisible. Even when he slouched at the edge of their group, out of place, longing to be part of it, but resenting the effort of fitting in, he was noticed. Big John. She wanted to help him, to give him a chance to feel like he belonged, but he hadn't the knack, and he blamed her for it. Blamed her for his unhappiness, his dissatisfaction, until she broke under the weight of his misery. And as she shrank into silence, faded into invisibility, he seemed to grow bigger, louder, until he was a constant presence, even when he wasn't around. She might be showering or combing her hair, cleaning or shopping, he would be looking over her shoulder, finding fault, whispering a solemn malediction of her transgressions. Until finally, even when she looked in the mirror at her own ghostly reflection, he was omnipresent, his fury like a black, pestilent swarm at her back.

But just as sunlight conveys solidity on invisible motes of dust, so the fire and fury of this night have reconstituted her. While he is eclipsed, she has taken form – she feels herself returning – the particles of herself that her husband caused to flee are returning into her.

'Aren't you afraid they'll catch you?' she calls after the jaunty man.

He glances over his shoulder, into the darkness made thick by the burning. 'Not me, girl. I've been invisible all me life.' He makes a sharp right at the school and is gone, and they are alone again.

'Don't you disobey me.'

The hairs rise on the back of her neck, but it is only from habit, a Pavlovian response. She hears a quaver of fear in the command, astonished to discover that it's been there all along. He tries to get up, but he is weak.

Around her, bricks and rubble. She bends to pick up a brick, and he shrinks from her. She could finish it. Make her protest and vanish. Rejoin the invisible.

She balances the brick in one hand and the tiger eye in the other. The husband licks his lips. His eyes widen, and she recognises the expression of terror.

'Order out of chaos,' she says, choosing the tiger eye.

She turns and walks away. Anger will come later: for now she feels light, unburdened.

A window explodes behind her, sending cascades of glass, musical, deadly, to the pavement. Laura is unharmed.

Something You Don't Have to Deserve

James Friel

Johnny Parrot finishes his set of Sinatra standards and stays onstage to call the bingo. He has a seventy-year old's face and a twenty-year old's hair, black beyond nature and quiffed into a cloud. Like his teeth and once-good tuxedo, the wig is a size too large. Nothing on Johnny looks as if it belonged to him first.

'Eyes down now, ladies and gentlemen, please and thank you. First ball up this evening is Duck and Dive, Number Five.'

His accent is deep scouse, his voice a rasp. You can hear his dentures slide, but when he sings he leaves Liverpool behind.

It is Sunday night at St Mary Martha's. The houselights are full on. The hall is in a hush. The grille comes down at the bar. No drinks are ordered or served. The bar staff gather behind the bar, stare out like sad animals at a zoo, and the waitresses take their usual break in the never busy Select Lounge.

Johnny can still be heard through the walls of the Select Lounge, a place of easy chairs, low tables and an old poster of a high-arching wave in Miami. Red flock pagodas float in neat order down the walls. The carpet is a sticky green.

Hands deep in her pinny pockets, Doreen counts her tips so far.

The new girl, Sam, fiddles with the strap of her halter-

103

top, wondering if bra-less was the best idea.

Terri, glum, not young and with this gammy eye, attends the smoke from her cigarette as if it were a joke she's been told too often.

This is the quiet time, the bingo lull. Next up, they'll be on the go all through the girl-singer and then the guest artiste and band until Last Orders, Please. There's never a comic on Sundays in case he blasphemes.

'Clickety-click: Sixty-Six,' says Johnny through the wall.

'Shixty-Shix!' says Terri, mocking him.

Sam laughs, but just the once.

Doreen sniffs, says nothing, loyal to Johnny. Terri Woodvine and this new girl, Sam, they work elsewhere weekdays, at Argos and at Boots, but St Mary Martha's is Doreen's only job, and, after fourteen years, she is expert at it. Five foot in her pumps, she zips between tables. Not much more to her than sinew, bone and a good stiff perm, regulars call her the whippet.

'I can carry twelve orders at any one time,' she tells Sam. 'I keep it all up here.' She taps her forehead sharply. Her perm, it does not move.

'I'll never be able to do that,' says Sam. This might be a confession. It might be a boast. 'And, ay, them trays are heavy, aren't they? Especially when you load them with pints. I've only got thin arms.'

Doreen smiles. 'Thin arms never stopped me.'

'Nothing does,' scoffs Terri. 'She hogs all the orders and leaves us scraps, and on Sunday scraps is all there is.'

Doreen studies the patterns nicotine makes on the Artex ceiling, thinking, 'Just rise above her, Doreen, rise above.'

'Are Sundays not much cop then?' Sam asks.

'You see, folk have all spent up the night before,' Doreen explains, being patient with Sam because she can't lose her temper with Terri.

Terri stretches her long legs, her one good asset. 'The tips are crap in here, full stop.'

Doreen says no more. End of an evening, even a Sunday, her pinny pockets are solid with silver. When she walks, she clanks. Let Terri Woodvine tut and moan. Let Terri Woodvine start up again about how they should share the good customers out and pool the tips because that's only fair, but what would Terri Woodvine know about being fair? Tips come from getting folk's orders double quick. Tips come from being liked and being trusted. Tips don't come from leading folk on and letting them down. Only this evening a lady – Double Martini Lemonade and a Stout – said to Doreen, 'I'd die of thirst in the desert before I gave Terri Woodvine my order. I don't know how you breathe the same air as her lying kind, Doreen, I truly don't. How is your little Martin anyway?'

As for the new girl, Sam, Doreen has professionally appraised her. Sam is young, big-boobed and slow. She'll stay a month or two and move on. No competition for Doreen, but – tiny smile – trouble there for Terri.

For Terri, Sundays just got thinner. The new girl, Sam, will serve fewer tables, take fewer orders and still make more from tips. Fellas will order double pints from Sam. They'll watch as she returns, those thin arms and great breasts trembling from carrying the heavy tray, spots of beer soaking that little halter-top. And fellas don't like Terri anyway. They remember her husband, Larry Woodvine. They don't forgive. And Terri's good legs count for little when she is otherwise flatly made, and a halter-top hangs on her like a dishcloth and now she has this gammy eye, her left, the pupil slowly dulling, as if it's gathering dust. If she closes her good eye, it's like looking at the world through a dusty jar.

The new girl, Sam, has taken in the club, the job, her fellow-waitresses, and dismissed them all without bitterness. Her black hair falls across her face. She rarely flicks it back to look out on a world that only looks on her to gawp at her solid breasts. Let it gawp. It's not her world, this: Sunday evenings, old folk, lonely fellas, Johnny Parrot crooning like a rusty wheel, trays of shorts and milds and double tops. It's not her life, this waiting-on. Like, right now, for instance, she's not thinking tips. She is looking at her hands. Her dead dad's hands, man's hands, she knows, but pale and immaculately kept. She is thinking nail varnish. She is thinking, *Happy Go Lucky Green*, *Pompeii Purple* or *Huckleberry Blush*? Which shade would look best in Tehran? Can you even wear nail varnish in Tehran?

'Get Up and Run,' says Johnny through the wall, 'Thirty-One.'

Somebody yells, 'House!' and Doreen snatches up her tray and tells Terri and Sam it's time to move.

Ten-thirty, the bar is shut for good. Behind the lowered grille, the bar staff mooch about, stacking up the empties.

Onstage, the guest artiste, a Malayan gentlemen, plump in a grey silk one-piece, plays *Una Paloma Blanca* and *The Real Slim Shady* on the electric organ. This is what folk like, what gets them up and dancing. This is what pushes Monday further back. It's what Johnny has failed to do this long while.

Instead, he joins Doreen, Terri and Sam in the Select Lounge on their longer second break.

'He often sits with us,' Doreen tells Sam, 'even though he's Talent and we're just Waiting-on.'

Doreen's Mam remembers Johnny Parrot years back, guesting at the Cavern in the days when his black hair was organic to his skull. Angular and tall, bent over a mike as if it were a hankie he was weeping into, he was Merseyside's own Johnny Ray. The hearts he broke. Two decades later, Doreen had done her own courting to his crooning at the Mecca, his voice then as sparkling as the glitterball above. She thought she'd see Johnny Parrot next on television – everyone did – but here he was, this star that should have shone, by rights, elsewhere, an Emcee at St Mary Martha's, probably earning no more than she was, a colleague now, almost a friend.

Doreen was treating herself to a sherry schooner. Terri and Sam have gone for Campari, ice, no soda. Johnny cradles a whisky sour, and watches as Sam and Terri count out their tips on the low table between them.

Doreen never counts out her tips, just empties her pinny pockets into her handbag and snaps it shut. Johnny registers the handbag's satisfying thump as she drops it to the floor.

'Another good night, Doreen? They can't beat you for the speed, the way you whiz about.'

'Keeps me trim, Johnny.' She pats her flat stomach, sips happily at her schooner.

'Ay, but folk don't always like to be rushed now, do they?' Johnny suggests mildly. 'They like to keep a glass standing before it's whipped away. Have time, you know, to digest.'

Doreen sniffs. 'Leave off ordering another drink, you mean. Cheap's what I call it.'

Loathe to agree, Terri admits Doreen is right. 'Women are the worst for lingering.'

Doreen nods. 'You get them as have one Baileys –'

'No,' interrupts Terri, 'not Baileys. Bacardi Breezer!'

'Because you get more to a glass with a Bacardi Breezer,' explains Sam who has learned this much already.

'Yes, you get them women as have one Bacardi Breezer and they spin that one drink out the whole evening.'

'Ah, but women, Doreen,' sighs Johnny, ever mellow, 'some women, they're not great drinkers.'

'Then why come to a club?' asks Terri. 'Why not stop at home?'

'I could care less,' says Doreen, 'whether they have one Bacardi Breezer or a bowl of cold porridge. They could sup what they like until Doomsday. What gets my giddy goat is calling me over every twenty minutes and sending me to the bar for glacé cherry after glacé cherry.'

'Because you don't have to pay for glacé cherries,' says Sam who has been caught out by this all evening.

'And not so much as a thank you, let alone a tip,' says Terri. 'Sometimes I drop it on the floor before I give it to them, and say, "Suck on that!"'

Terri Woodvine always goes that bit too far. Terri was bar staff once. She'd wear low necks and did a lot of bending – although she had nothing to show, but freckles. She only served the men, who thought her desperate but would flirt back just to get quick service. Then she met that soft lad, Larry Woodvine, had baby Callum, stayed at home looking after them both until Hillsborough Stadium happened – ninety-four dead in the end and hundreds injured – and Larry was gone from the face of the earth, no warning, no nothing, and she was back fending for herself, and Callum. Waiting-on's a demotion. She's not much cop. She walks about with this bovine tread, gives out the wrong change, mixes up or clean forgets an order, has her thumb in a drink when she puts it down.

On the low table in front of Sam is a lake of silver coins. In front of Terri is a puddle of copper ones and a few lonely twenty-pence pieces. Terri shuffles her tips back into her pinny pocket. Sam goes on counting hers. Doreen inhales her schooner of sherry as if it were a rose she was holding by its stalk. Johnny sips at his whisky sour. In the main hall, the Malayan gentleman launches into *Hot Love* with a salsa beat, and the audience bellow the chorus.

Sam yawns, stretches, pushes out her profitable breasts, lets them fall, and yawns again. Doreen lights up her single fag of the day, savours its poisons. Terri undoes her strappy sandals, rests her naked feet on the low table so they can breathe a bit. Johnny looks on, admiring women, their easy ways when they forget themselves. Under his breath, he sings *To All the Girls I've Loved*.

'Is that Julio Iglesias you're singing?'

'Julio has been known to sing it, too. Are you a fan, Doreen, of Signor Iglesias?'

It's Terri who answers. 'Oh, he's greasy-slick, he is. Foreign men, they leave me cold.'

'Leave you alone, more like,' says Johnny, grinning.

Doreen sniggers, but Johnny means no harm, only to tease. Terri is so dour at times. They live next door to one another and rarely talk. He doesn't like her anymore than most, but he pities her when he hears folk call her The Widow and then either laugh or spit at her behind her back. And then he is fascinated by her foggy eye. These months past he has been watching how a cloud has slubbered over her left pupil. He'd like to reach out, touch it, press his finger soft against it and wipe it clean of dust. Funny how a woman takes you.

'I like DJ Nader and Reza Sadeghi,' says Sam. They look blank at her, but in Iran, Sam knows, everyone moves to the music of Reza Sadeghi. 'He's got polio, Reza Sadeghi. He walks with a stick, and sings like there's a bird trapped in his throat.'

Johnny nods. 'Disability's no bar to a singing career. Look at Jane Froman. *With a Song in My Heart.* Sang it all through the war in a wheelchair. No legs, bless her, but lovely shoulders.'

'If you're talking music,' says Doreen, 'my idea of heaven is an afternoon alone, kiddies in school, housework done, telly off, feet up, a saucerful of chocolate Hobnobs, and Michael Bublé washing over me full pelt.'

Sam wants to barf, but goes back to counting her tips. Every tip she counts brings her one step closer to being elsewhere. Sometimes, in her head, she's there already.

'Have you not done counting them tips?' Terri asks, peeved.

'I've twelve quid here.'

'That's quite good for a Sunday,' says Terri, who's

made three. 'How've you done, Doreen, or aren't you saying?'

Doreen never tells exact. She lifts her handbag an inch from the floor, weighs it, and looks ahead as if the total is written on the air. 'Oh, enough for a primus.'

'What's one of them?'

'A primus, Sam, is like a stove you have for camping. We have this camper van, Allan and me. Five kids, holidays don't come cheap. The camper van's a lifesaver. Come summer, we climb in and go all over. Rhyl. Riverton Pike. Lake District. Everywhere. Camper vans are a sight cheaper than hotels, and comfier.'

'I had a friend had a camper van,' Terri puts in.

'Did you? Camper vans are very economic, but we do need a primus. The cost of all seven of us eating at a Little Chef is frightening.'

'I had a friend work at a Little Chef,' Terri puts in again. 'That one on the road to Knowsley. I wouldn't eat their salads.'

'Would you not? So hence the primus. It'll save us loads.'

'There used to be a club out Knowsley way,' Johnny tells them.

'Where's Knowsley?' asks Sam.

'Primus apart, we've got everything in that camper van we'll ever need.'

'The Silver Bowl,' says Johnny. 'I sang weeknights there. Closed now. There's not much to Knowsley, singing-wise.'

'We've all the comforts of home in our camper van. Curtains, matching duvets, television, rug, terracotta sink and shower.'

'I wonder how you fit the kids in,' says Terri.

Doreen sniffs. 'I work hard to furnish my family with life's pleasures.'

Blood in the air, thinks Johnny as Terri sniffs back.

Terri doesn't work for life's luxuries, but for its basics; to feed the gas, pay off the catalogue and the loans, buy shoes for her boy – not even the trainers he's begging her for, just shoes, ones she can afford.

'We're a very close family, Sam,' Doreen continues breezily. 'Anyone'll tell you that. Our Julie's thirteen. She's not out drugging it or drinking or having boyfriends. We've only got to say 'Colwyn Bay' and she's first in the van with her iPod. That's why I'm here. That's why I'm on earth. My family is my life.'

Every last word of this is a dart thrown at Terri Woodvine. Terri wants to wince, but she'll not lose face and so she gulps at her Campari without pleasure.

Johnny's nodding. He's known Doreen years, not well, but he remembers her starting when St Mary Martha's was converted from the church school into a club, and he, in the last stretch of his prime, became Emcee, a stage of his own at last. Doreen had been saving to get married and had her eye on a flat in Grafton Street. He'd asked how many kids she'd wanted. She'd said four, one for each corner of the room.

'Strictly speaking,' she tells Sam, 'I do have four. The fifth child, our Martin, he's not mine.'

Terri has decided to do up her strappy sandals. She needs something to do with her hands. She needs somewhere to look and seem occupied.

'He's my nephew. My brother Eric's child. Eric died' – and Doreen can't help but flick her eyes at Terri – 'at Hillsborough. My brother was one of the ones that died. At Hillsborough.'

Doreen's eyes threaten to spill with tears so Sam bows her head rather than watch, her own eyes lost behind her black fringe. She remembers Hillsborough like something she did at school. Her form teacher's dad had died at Hillsborough. There had been a collection and a special assembly. Her class had made a floral wreath out of tissue paper.

'Our Eric was up at the front, first through the tunnel that day. He wouldn't have been that far from the fence. He died standing up. We know that much.'

Doreen knows more than this. She sees her brother's face, the wrong colour, eyes like spoiled eggs, tongue extended –

'Now, don't take on, Doreen,' says Johnny, daring to pat her knee.

Doreen recovers, waves her hands to cool her face, says, 'Me, I don't take on, Johnny, I'm not that sort. I'm not that type. There's other people with sadder tales to tell than me.' And she risks a longer look at Terri Woodvine, but Terri, sandals strapped, is looking at the poster of a high-arching wave in Miami. What if it came, a wave like that, and washed her clean away? She'd not struggle. She'd go with it.

'And if our Eric dying that way wasn't bad enough,' says Doreen, 'my sister-in-law, Maureen, she was pregnant at the time. Very glam is Maureen. Used to work here behind the bar, and then did the cloakroom.'

Johnny remembers a cleavage in a lace-up blouse, a lipsticky mouth and giant bobble earrings.

'The marriage wasn't working anyway, we all knew that. She hadn't wanted the kiddie before, and she didn't want it after. And then little Martin was born, poor mite, and they told her, complications. He was damaged, you know, coming out. They said, would you like to hold him, and she goes, oh no, keep the little bastard away from me. I could've wept. I did. She had money coming, and she emigrated not long after. Canada, if you please. Winnipeg! Pakistani lover a third her age. Left little Martin in care. Dropped him off at Social Services like a bag of dirty washing.'

'Grief takes folks all kinds of ways,' says Johnny, stealing a glance at Terri. For weeks back then, he would stand in his pantry and listen to Terri Woodvine next door weeping in hers.

'I said to our Alan, hang about. I'm not having that, a

little boy in a home and he's done no wrong. I'll have him. I call him son and he calls me Mam and who's to say we've both not the right. I love kids. Mother the whole world, if I could.'

'It does you credit, Doreen,' says Johnny. 'Really it does.'

'I couldn't go off to Canada,' says Sam, but she thinks, I will go off to Iran. Persia, it used to be called, where the carpets come from.

'And what about you, Terri?' asks Doreen, and the question is out almost before she knows it, 'Have you never thought of leaving?'

Everyday, that's what Terri wants to say, but she's ready for Doreen. 'No, I stay put. Here's home, isn't it? And there's our Callum.'

'Doesn't he miss his dad?' Doreen can't resist. 'I mean, seems we all lost someone we know that day.'

'Callum doesn't even mention his dad these days, thank you. Most folk leave us alone.'

That isn't true, but it's enough to shame Doreen who nods and, pursed-lipped, sips at her sherry.

Johnny remembers an early drink at St Mary Martha's – the sun a bright fog through the dirty windows – and lingering to watch the match against Sheffield on the TV rolled into the Select Lounge whenever Liverpool played live.

The match had begun normal enough, but there was something troubling and unmentioned happening whenever the camera passed over the Leppings Lane End of the stadium. A riot brewing or just hooligans, he'd thought until the game was stopped, the pitch filling with bodies splayed out or being carried away, and others running about and standing before the Leppings Lane End, their mouths square with agony.

Thousands of Liverpool fans had been pushed through a narrow tunnel into the already packed central pens. The people already there were being crushed against the fencing by the weight of the crowd pressing forward, unaware of what was happening. The police, stewards and ambulance service were inadequate, inept, overwhelmed. Uninjured fans helped as best they could, some tearing down advertising hoardings to act as makeshift stretchers only to be arrested by the uncomprehending police.

The sad miracle was how the Select Lounge slowly began to fill, people coming unbidden from off the streets and the houses roundabout, sensing something terrible was happening to their kind. The television played on and on, the commentary unable to deal with what the camera was revealing. They watched fans break through the cordon to ferry the injured to waiting ambulances only to be beaten back by the police, the dead and dying left unattended, while the innocent were coshed and wrestled to the ground. 'That's our Damien,' one woman shouted as the camera zoomed in on a young lad in trackies, knelt down and vomiting on the grass.

Later, the houselights up full, the TV still on and no one watching but for a few who would call out across the club whatever developments were being reported. There was no bingo that night, no music. Those who came just stood at the bar or sat at a table, hardly speaking.

Terri Woodvine was one of them, little Callum next to her, no more than five, with his dad's ginger hair and soft green eyes. Larry Woodvine was at the match. Have you heard anything, she'd ask, anything at all? Apart from that, she said little else, sat unmoving as people came up, stroked her cheek, stroked little Callum's, told her there was hope, there was always hope, that no news was good news, and Larry would turn up.

The priest arrived, breathless from a hospice some place else. He said a sort of mass right there where the artistes usually stood, and Johnny sang *Ave Maria*, and noticed Terri Woodvine singing with him, mouthing the words she didn't know, little Callum next to her. Odd to see a child sit so long and not fidget.

But then Larry had been the quiet sort, too, something not right about his slack mouth, something absent from his eyes. One summer Larry had dug a big hole in his back garden. Making a swimming pool, he said. All he managed was a muddy hole the length of the lawn that filled with stagnant water. Johnny could smell the scummy water, green and noxious, from his own house – even with the windows closed. Larry Woodvine was always strange.

Johnny wonders when it was Terri stopped wearing her wedding ring. On her finger there isn't even a mark where it would have been.

Sam is thinking rings, too. The one she wears is Diamonique, opal and gold-effect. She wasn't measured for it, but he had remembered her hands perfectly.

His name is Naf. Her mother sniggers at the name, but he has eyes like tadpoles, black and lively, swimming in milk. His lashes are inches long. His voice turns her into fur being stroked, warm and softly bristling. She met him at *Charmers* on Hardman Street. They will have the most beautiful children.

Right now, it is 2.00 am in Tehran. He is asleep in white sheets. He says his family only ever has white sheets. His father is a doctor. Naf will be an engineer. Below his bedroom there is a courtyard the colour of ice cream. Sometimes, she can float off and be in bed beside him, close and warm.

Her mother worries. Home is home, her mam says. It's where you're born, where you belong, something yours by right. And if it's been too long since Naf has written, telephoned or texted – like all this week – then she thinks, well, maybe where you're born is where you belong, and something in her settles or dies: she can't tell which.

Here the world is so small and cramped, it's hard to see beyond it. There are people in the club tonight her age, sitting with their mams and dads or the fiancés or fiancées who live in the next street, soon-to-be-husbands and soon-to-be-wives who've only known each other.

Trevor Stokes is one such. He had given Sam her first love bite when she was twelve. Head Boy at her school, his future wife had been Head Girl, and now Elaine was in hospital, a hysterectomy at twenty-seven. He had the same features still, Roman nose and a tiny mouth, but already an older man's face was thickening around them. Earlier, when he and Sam had spoken at the bar, the love bite from years ago had tingled on her neck – or was that Naf turning in his sleep all those miles away and sighing?

Love stretches out. It can find out where we live. It can tell us we are home or it can tell us how very far from home we are. And, as with Sam's love bite remembering itself or Naf's sleep-warm breath on her neck, so, perhaps, another woman, in Canada, pulling at the bobble earrings that are her trademark, might feel that deeper tug of a child she has left behind. She had only wanted to be in a place where the world happened happily for once. Cold Winnipeg isn't home, and yet she stays. And, somewhere nearer by, in Knowsley, a woman, watching TV from her single bed, hums the tune to *Body and Soul*, the words, and why the tune comes at all, a mystery. And so, too, a man, nameless now and stained as Cain was stained, closes his eyes against the orange streetlights. Tonight he lies in a shop doorway in East Kilbride, but he no longer knows where he is. His world now comes without a map. He had only ever had a vague idea of geography. In his half-sleep, his nervous fingers forage the cold air as if tunnelling deep and down into the black soil until he reaches the end of earth, where, surely, there's a home at last.

This may be all that each of them in their dispeopled kingdoms knows of home; this sigh, a sudden wrench, a match flaring in the dark: signs and gestures, remote flickerings that beckon them, tell them where they each, at heart, belong, and yet they each resist as if such knowledge is something they somehow don't deserve.

Midnight, the slow exit.

People hang about, singing the old songs – *Don't Fence Me In, My Heart Will Go On, Been Around the World (and I Can't Find My Baby)*. Lovely voices, some of them, a fresh surprise at the night's end, the men caramel-toned and deep, and even the blowsiest of women might sing sweet as a nun.

The whole evening should have been like this, people coming together, finding themselves at home in song. They'd sing another hour or more if the waitresses didn't take away their glasses and the ashtrays, telling them nicely to go home so they can wipe the tables down.

Some dawdle in the car park, calling out farewells. See you, honey, see you, cheery bye, be safe and see you soon, they coo, one to the other as they part, the words rising and falling like birds settling for the night. The streetlamps turn their faces orange.

The waitresses don't say good-bye to one another. They don't even think to do so. There's no ill will. They're heading home.

Doreen, high-heeled now, clacks her way to the door, nods to the bar staff in their coats and washing the last of the empties. She calls goodnight to folk as she passes them in the car park, snapping each syllable out, more abrupt than cheery. She's on her own time now. Allan is waiting in the camper van.

She climbs in the back. Little Martin's there, shoes undone, happy to see her, dribbling. She ties his laces neatly and wipes the spit that hangs like a pearl from his chin and sucks her finger. It tastes of Martin, of childhood, crisps and Polo Mints.

'How'd you get on?' her husband asks.

'Not bad. For a Sunday. Eighteen-fifty. We've enough for that Primus.'

'It'll do us a treat in Bala, will that,' says Alan, and starts up the camper van.

Doreen belts herself in, pulls Martin close, admires the back of Alan's neck, the way the night and the streetlamps stripe the camper van's interior orange and black.

Her second home, this camper van, a miracle how all seven of them will roll along in it through Wales, the Lakes, the Peaks; the world reeling past, purple moors, mirrored water, hills that spread and lose themselves in fog, and Doreen, Alan and the kids at the centre of all this movement, speeding along, safe and still.

'Scratch that primus,' says Alan. 'I was thinking, if we got the right attachment, waited another month, we could have a microwave in here. What d'you think to that?'

He half turns in the driver's seat so as to catch her smile widen at the half she can see of his.

Sam won't be walking home alone. Trevor Stokes has offered to come with her.

'You live off Park Road, don't you? You have to cut through the back of the old Leo's. I don't like to think of you going down there in the dark.'

On their way home they talk of all sorts. They talk about his wife, Naf, Tehran, a courtyard the colour of ice cream, and how there'd be nothing wrong if, one night after Trevor has visited Elaine in hospital, he stopped by at *Charmers* on Hardman Street for a drink and a dance maybe, and so they reach the back of the old supermarket where it's dark and there's glass on the asphalt and potholes here and there and homeless guys living in the doorways, and so he takes her arm for safety's sake and he steadies her.

Terri walks home with Johnny.

They don't often do this, but Johnny thinks his company will make up for some hurt he witnessed and did not prevent.

Terri's thinking how first thing she'll go upstairs to Callum's room. He's at his gran's, same as every weekend so Terri can work evenings. She just wants to smell his room, breathe it in deep. He is why she is on earth.

She's about to say 'Ta-ra,' and leave Johnny at her gate, but he coughs and asks what no one else has asked in years: 'Do you ever hear from Larry?'

'No,' she answers back. 'I don't.'

That'd be that. Her hand is on the gate. She could just go inside, forget he asked such a thing. There's a packet of Jaffa Cakes she's hidden from Callum in the washing machine. She deserves a treat, but Johnny is a neighbour, one of the few she suspects is kind. He's cared enough to ask.

'I expect I never shall hear now. He never went to that match that day. He never went to any match. Home or away. Not that day. Not any day. Not ever. Just pretended. God knows where he went instead. He's not here to ask, is he?'

'No,' says Johnny. 'No, he's not.'

'I think he's wandering some place else. Nameless. Homeless. Who else would take him in, but me? If he did turn up, I'd not open the door. Not now. Remember when he dug that hole in our back garden?'

Johnny nodded. It was the summer after his Nerys died.

'He wasn't building a swimming pool, like he said. That'd be stupid. And he was even stupider. He was digging his way to Australia. He thought you could dig a hole deep enough and there he'd be. That's all he had to do. Dig a hole and he'd be elsewhere.'

'Ah, Terri, he wasn't well. You can see that now.'

'Me? I saw it then.'

She stares straight at him, one eye glistening and direct, the other opaque, no real colour in the orange streetlight. He wants to touch it.

'I knew he wasn't dead, just getting softer and softer in the head. But I loved it, thinking he might be, you know,

119

dead. It was better than what I ended up doing, going about alone and sticking up photocopies of his face on lampposts and post-office walls like he was some dog I lost. Better him dead with all those others, God forgive me, a whole city mourning for him maybe. And I loved it. The attention. That night at the club, people coming up, sorry for my loss, angry on my behalf. The bouquets next morning. The money pushed through the doors in envelopes. The picture of him in the papers along with all the other proper dead. I sucked it all up. I felt like I belonged. Now they hate me for it. I've never been much liked. Even at school I sat alone at a double desk.'

There's this awkward duck and dive as he makes to kiss her. He pulls back even as he thinks of it, cocks his head and swallows so she has no idea a kiss was what he was after, thinks he was merely shifting his dentures, the way old men do. He looks away, looks back and she's gone inside. Once, he'd been more dapper.

He glances up through the orange streetlight at the sky struggling to be dark, and at the stars, if he could see them, and the little they have to do with him.

At The Silver Bowl in Knowsley they'd had a ceiling lit with stars. He'd worn an orange tuxedo. The night Matt Munro first appeared on *Opportunity Knocks* instead of him, the sky through the backstage window was all purple and rain. He'd opened with *Luck, Be a Lady* and ended with *Body and Soul*, singing the last to a woman in a dirndl with horse-teeth. It happened, a face in the audience singled itself out, held you like an anchor as you swanned about the stage. He saw her just that once from the stage, but he'd married Nerys who'd been the very spit of her one year after. It's what you do: if you can't live the life you sing about, you get as close as you can to the melody. You hum along.

Nerys had the best of Johnny. He hadn't always been that fond or kind.

He's straight to bed, no messing. He can wash his face

come morning. He wakes early most days. Nerys wakes him, thoughts of her, the lack of her when he reaches out. All his married life, and it was only when she died that she became a woman he loved with the kind of love you sing about in songs.

They used to keep their dentures in the same pint pot by the bed. The week she died, he threw hers out; the pint pot, too. Now, his dentures swim alone in a whisky tumbler.

The orange streetlamp shines in and glitters them. They smile back at him as his tongue traces his gums, and he sings to her, for she's never that far away, hovering about the earth, close by, not attached as such, at home nowhere else but where he is.

I've Got You Under My Skin; *Desafinado*; *I Get Along Without You Very Well*; *Say it's Only a Paper Moon; Every Time We Say Goodbye*; his voice is cracked, the words a mumble, the lyrics of one song stumbling into another. There's not much sense to it by sleep's edge, that sudden fall into the dark, but there's the heart he puts into it, and the way it sounds in his head, the slow silky dip and soar of his ideal voice. He dreams then. He dreams he lies with his head between Nerys' legs. He dreams he's home.

A Different Sky

Dinesh Allirajah

The story had been told around Nelson so many times, it had come to feel like a memory of his own. So he was able to picture the cloudless sky, underlined by the tops of Sefton Park's steepling pine trees, with the smashed and blackened windows of the Palm House rising to meet his eyeline. Everyone at the wedding could recall the photographer, Mervyn, lifting four-month-old Nelson out of the way of the group shot, but that view of the blue was his alone and it remained in sharp focus, eighteen years and one summer later.

Lined up among these improbable memories was the cab ride from the registry office to the park. Nelson, dozing off to the taxi's rockabye rhythms, wouldn't have heard the conversation his mum and dad had with Mervyn, who had jumped in with them. It usually prefaced the anecdote, though, so he'd learned the script.

'Weather's a bit of a pain,' Mervyn suggested, saucer-sized glasses bulging his eyes even as they sat in their natural downcast position.

'Could be a touch warmer, I guess,' said Mum, 'but it's fine, really.'

'Hmm,' Mervyn put her straight, 'I suppose the happy couple and the guests'll be pleased to have this blue sky – but it doesn't make for very good photographs. You lose people with the blue, see. I'd have preferred it cloudy.'

'What? Like, grey?' Dad asked.

'White cloud would do. They'll notice it when they get

123

their pictures back, that's all.'

Twenty minutes later, a cluster of cabs having reassembled the wedding party above the galloping squiggle of a stream known as the Fairy Grotto, Mervyn had found a possible solution to his lighting problems. By gathering everyone together at the foot of a sheer grassy bank, he could ensure a mainly green backdrop and negate the clear sky. It was still proving troublesome, though. The bride and groom, Judy and Will, were arty types who saw their wedding as a celebration on behalf of a pick'n'mix, ragbag, surrogate family of DJs, poets, dealers, dancers, visual artists and unsigned bands. They'd even postponed the disco to the following night because they, and half the guests, had tickets to see Sun Ra's Arkestra at the Bluecoat Arts Centre, following the reception. So these shots had to work because Mervyn wasn't booked in to capture them relaxed and candid at the do. Arranging them into bride's or groom's side was a non-starter; the bohemian fashions meant hardly any dark suits or pastels to enable Judy and Will to stand out in the group picture; and now the slope was causing people at the back to stumble, shoving the whole lot of them forward and cutting off their feet. Finally, Mervyn got them all still, together and framed, but someone had stuck a baby's car seat in the foreground.

Mervyn swooped down in front of the tripod and clamped his hands either side of Nelson's ribs. 'Can I move this?' he asked, carrying the car seat over to where he'd piled his empty cases.

The guests giggled like the backseat gang on a school coach trip. A voice called out, 'But that's a person too, Merv!'

Mervyn didn't respond. At least he'd be able to say he made everyone look as if they'd been having a good time.

Nelson rocked, alone in his seat, and the sky's immense seaside blue swayed and nodded back.

★

He looked up at it again now, as he sat on the steps leading to the apartment block where St Luke's, the bombed-out church, used to be. Rather than get off the bus at Lime Street, he'd decided to walk through town to get to the station. He'd said his goodbyes at home after breakfast and taken his bags out to the park. He found the same vantage point he'd been given by Mervyn back in 1990, and the pine trees were green, the Palm House windows now clear and shining, and the sky was still no good for photos. It was there above him, too, when he walked down Lark Lane and got an 82 bus on Aigburth Road, and it stayed with him now. *He* was the one leaving it behind.

★

The Concert Hall at the Bluecoat had the floorboard creaks, wheezy electrics and rattling windows better suited to a church jumble sale than a concert by eighteen intergalactic jazz troubadours.

'Are you's all here to see Sun Rraaaa?' bellowed the compere, one of the star DJs on Toxteth Community Radio, the pirate station.

Two hundred pairs of feet stomped on the raked seating unit and it jolted forward some three centimetres. Cheers choked up what remained of the air supply after the rake had sliced the room into two diagonals.

'And have you's got all of his records?'

About sixty pairs of feet stomped this time and, amid the cheers, 'Yeah, why not?' could be made out, along with 'Probably' and 'Some.'

Abi glanced down at the pram. Nelson hadn't stirred. The usher, who'd allowed her to sit with the pram below one of the windows rather than on the rake, mouthed, 'Is he OK?' and winked at Abi's thumbs-up. Max was sitting with

Will's best man, Mickey, in the main seating block and he also turned an anxious head to check on the baby. Abi smiled and gave him an amazed shrug, which he returned.

They'd had a perfunctory debate, during the wedding reception, about whether they were expecting too much of Nelson to make it through the concert after a gruelling day. Abi had lobbed up the words, 'I *could* just take him home,' and Max had offered a weak parry, saying, 'No, it's OK, I will,' but neither was fooled. They'd already missed Malcolm X Day at the Philharmonic when Nelson was ten days old, and Sun Ra wasn't going to pass them by, especially after they'd paid £3.50 each for the tickets.

During the Arkestra's second set, Nelson woke up. The cue came from the brass section, which had been striking up raucous conversations all evening. This exchange was particularly rasping, a musical rendition of a bar room brawl. Abi automatically reached down to stroke her son's head and felt his hand at once pushing away and grabbing hold. She unstrapped him and lifted him onto her lap. Nelson had on his crumpled waking face, its muscles in docile paroxysms. This gave him eyebrows like arches on a viaduct, and cheeks that puffed one at a time, as if passing a ball to each other. As Abi looked at him, Sun Ra's face came into view over Nelson's left shoulder, from behind the Bechstein Grand. Framed together, the expressions worn by the four-month-old Liverpudlian, possibly in need of a feed, and the millennia-old visitor from Saturn, at the piano keyboard, matched one another dimple for dimple. Maybe, Abi thought, Ra wasn't really the alien he claimed to be but someone who'd simply taken eighty-odd years to get used to being a baby. Then again, as Nelson turned his head towards the music and snuggled into her chest, maybe his had been the extraterrestrial visitation in February, beamed through the frankly not purpose-built portal of her womb, shortly after Mandela strolled through the prison gates. She'd tell him that, later in the night, he'd danced with June Tyson, the Arkestra's stately vocalist, when the musicians', orange and gold kaftans got up to sashay around the stage, chanting, 'We travel the spaceways, from planet to planet.' Tyson had spotted the child but their dance was more of a solemn game of peek-a-boo than anything else. Regardless, the family folklore had been written by the time they'd spilled onto the Bluecoat's eighteenth-century cobbled courtyard.

'They really wanna re-name the Bluey now, though, y'know,' Mickey said as they walked up to the taxi rank at the corner of Chinatown.

'How's that?' Max said, steering the pram past a puddle of Saturday night sick.

Mickey stopped to re-light his spliff, which he held with the flame pointing into the palm of his hand, 'British officer style,' as he called it. He wafted at the smoke drifting in the pram's direction and looked across to Abi. 'This OK?' he added, pointing at Nelson.

'We're out in the open air, Mick,' said Abi, but she hurried herself to walk a few metres in front of the aroma.

Mickey returned to his theme, 'Yeah, dred – call it the Sun Ra Centre or, y'know, thingyo the road – re-name School Lane...'

'Sun Ra Lane?' Max offered.

'Arkestra Avenue! What d'you reckon?'

'Not really an avenue, though, is it?'

'You know what I mean,' he grinned, 'Twat.'

'You have a point,' said Max, 'Reckon you could write to them yuppies who the Council sold the city centre to.'

'Nah, but this is it, matey – *this* is where a city starts, not when some bored Tory decides to build a few wine bars. See your lad there? He'll have this all the way to his grave, no offence. They should give us all our own cemetery – 'Here lies the dudes that saw Sun Ra at the Bluey, June 9th 1990,' and then a big smiley face at the bottom to confuse all the ravers.'

★

St George's Hall, like a surprise guest waiting behind a stage curtain, was draped in the usual multicoloured banners advertising whatever festival was going on this week. A billboard on the side of the Holiday Inn Hotel bid a 'Welcome To Liverpool's New Students – arriving fashionably late to the party of the century!' Nelson watched some of those arriving as he strolled towards the main station entrance, and he was now able to read that the St George's Hall bunting proclaimed the 'Culture 2008 Freshers' Festival.' He wondered about the reception given to his mum and dad when they'd washed up here in the 1980s.

'Being a student? Studying for an *arts* degree in Thatcher's Britain?' Dad had once said, 'It was only the miners, the gays and the Rastas keeping us at the back of the queue to face the firing squad.'

'Them, and the Scousers,' Mum added, like they'd been rehearsing their routine, 'so I guess we came to the right place.'

★

Max had been right there with Abi for the night feeds in the first few weeks. He'd perform hushed cheerleading duties as Abi took the strain, and then he'd rock Nelson off to sleep if the milk hadn't knocked him out. As Abi and Nelson relaxed into their part of the routine, Max simply relaxed. By the end of the summer, he was sleeping through the night. They'd swap round, he assured Abi, once Nelson was on formula milk. When the time came, when the crying and Abi's elbows in his ribs jolted him from under the covers into the November chill, Max found he couldn't manage without accessories. With Nelson and the bottle in the crook of one arm, he'd use the other to butter a slice of toast, make a cup of tea and scribble a few verses. If there was something good on TCR, he had the complete kit.

The best pirate station in Britain, according to *The Face* magazine, usually stayed on air till four in the morning. Tonight, though, the nightshift DJs seemed to have set their sights on making it all the way through to the breakfast show. They were celebrating 'Jimi Hendrix Day,' marking the twentieth anniversary of his death and 'reclaiming him as a pivotal figure for Black music.'

This, mused Max as Nelson took leisurely gulps from the bottle, was Liverpool. Striking dockers argued about Trotsky and the Kronstadt garrison over their pints; young parents took their babies and toddlers with them to throw their Poll Tax bills on public bonfires; and community radio DJs came out with sociological tracts about Jimi Hendrix in amongst the tunes and in between tokes on what they were obviously smoking. Maybe people like that existed in the rest of the country but, here, it was the culture, a radical conga line down Arkestra Avenue.

'We did the culture conga down Arkestra Avenue,' he told Nelson, 'the culture conga down the avenue with – down the lane with Sun Ra, con-gah. We did the culture conga down the lane with Sunra.' Max patted the couch beside him, feeling for a pen.

When he finally sat down to write, having taken off his dressing gown to wrap Nelson up and lay him out on the couch, Max had given up trying to compose a poem. Instead, he rooted in a KwikSave bag and brought out a John Menzies lined exercise book with 'FUNDING PROPOSAL' written on the cover. The Jimi Hendrix special was working through practically everything the Experience released, along with Peel Sessions with a young Stevie Wonder sitting in on drums and the late Band of Gypsys sound, with its heavier emphasis on funk. There were influences, acolytes and disciples too: Max heard the Isley Brothers and Miles Davis in the mix, and the MTV generation's take on the black rock trio, Living Colour. The modern digital recording and pressing gave Vernon Reid's guitar more metal than the other music on the show could generate, and it woke Abi up.

'Hello. Is he OK? What's this?' she had a perturbed singsong in her voice, too sleepy to sound the gruff adult.

'Living Colour,' Max opted for winningly perky, 'I mean, it's OK, appeals more to the dogma than the soul, I reckon.'

'What's *this*?' Abi repeated, with a sweep of a hand that managed to take in the radio, lamp, half-eaten toast, Nelson on the couch and Max in writing mode.

'Doing that proposal – me and Will got that meeting on Thursday.'

Abi turned the radio down and completed the conversation with the back of her head. 'He needs to be back in his cot.'

'OK. In a minute,' said Max, opening the exercise book.

The DJs had played *Machine Gun* and *The Star-Spangled Banner* and called for immediate peace in the Persian Gulf, and Nelson was still snuffling the couch cushions. Max threshed at the page with his pen, scribbling beneath the heading, 'Questions For Charterhouse.'

Charterhouse Estates had a Chief Executive, shareholders and a number of staff. Some had moved, or were commuting, from London; others had been recruited in the eight months since the property developers paid £7million for a triangle of land in the heart of the city centre. The purchase made them landlords to the garden sun-trap and architectural and human ruins of St Luke's, downtown through the thrifty coffee shop cool of Bold Street, along Hanover Street to the monumental redbrick shell of the old Bridewell, in and out of Duke Street's late-night shebeens and the bars and wrecked warehouses of the rope walk streets, up to The Blackie, a cathedral of socialist community arts in another former church, and every step of a culinary journey through Chinatown. The avowed purpose of what otherwise seemed a fire-sale was that the area would be transformed into a 'Cultural Industries Quarter.' For all the specifics of its enterprise, the company's name had taken on a heftier meaning. Whether an Ice Age, Enlightenment or Great War, 'Charterhouse' was the thing happening to the city, to its artists: to withstand the onset of Charterhouse, one had to come to terms with Charterhouse. So it was that Max and Will detected that they and most of their friends were suddenly being addressed, not as arty-farty lefties on the dole, but as Cultural Industries. It was a short step from this unfamiliar sensation to effervescent plotting to take over a disused warehouse and build, like Hendrix and his Electric Lady studios, an artist-run utopia with live jazz and foreign cinema.

'How will public funding interfere with the artists' ability to control the means of their production?' Max wrote. Nelson gave a cough. One of the nightshift team played the Hendrix song *Freedom*, then had a brief on-air debate with himself about whether he'd played it a couple of hours earlier. 'How do we go from being the pariahs to being the Politburo? How do you impose a business model on people who exist by taking cash in hand, by fiddling the dole, the housing and the 'leccy; who are radio pirates, Poll Tax avoiders, squatters; whom the police see as potential rioters; whom employees do not see at all when they see their Liverpool 8 postcodes; who have to take their babies to meetings because they can't afford nurseries and they can't find a crèche?'

Nelson understood that this wasn't his cot but he wasn't in bed next to Mum either. There was a light on, music was playing and Dad was scribbling so it had to be the morning. As with any other morning, he needed his drum toy. He decided to point this out to Dad.

★

Max had already met an old college friend, Fatima, while he waited for Will by the steps of St Luke's. He'd dropped the exercise book and all his papers for the meeting when she'd grabbed his hands and swung him round in a dance. She'd also given Nelson a kiss and told him he was blessed. Max saw Will on the other side of Leece Street, by the hole-in-the-wall 'Dog Burger' bar, so he placed a clenched fist high in the air as a salute. Will crossed the road carefully, then skipped the rest of the way, pumping both his fists.

'Yes, yes, yes, yes, yes, YEESS!' he yelled at Max.

'Oh my God!' Max shouted back, 'I can't believe it – finally!'

'Eleven years, man – e-lev-en *years.*'

They stood and laughed in each other's face. 'I really can't believe it,' Max said again. Will ran on the spot. Max took Nelson out of the pram and raised him up towards the sky, like a scene from the adverts for Gillette.

Nelson hadn't been sure about the lady kissing him – she seemed very kind but most strangers would have given him a sweet in those situations – but he did like this flying. He could see the red, gold and green stripes on Will's hat, and the fact that Dad's hair was shorter than his own, and both observations made him laugh. When he came to rest on Dad's shoulders, he could now see the top of another man's head and there was hardly any hair there at all, just two grey patches at the sides. The man was walking past Dad and Will but he stopped for a moment, and his stiff grey suit made their denims seem even more soft and crumpled.

'Great day, isn't it, lads?' the man said.

Will adjusted his voice to register his upbringing rather than his residence. 'Absolutely, sir. Ding-dong, the witch is dead – now if we can just find a way to get rid of Bush and get out of the Gulf, we'll be sorted.'

★

There was a rumble of sound coming from the space between the Gent's and the Cornish Pasty stand on Lime Street station's concourse. Nelson wandered through a slalom track of students, each plugged into an iPod and stooped over a text message. None was paying any attention to the source of the sound, a crew of teenage rappers in 'Welcome – Wilkommen – Bienvenue!' T-shirts, sharing a microphone on a tinny PA.

'Star of music hall and screen,' spat one of the crew, 'Arthur Askey reigned supreme.'

After a few more bars, Nelson understood that he was hearing a history of Liverpool in rap. A pimped-up chorus of *Ferry Cross The Mersey* broke up the verses. Added to the mix, and regularly drowning out the words, were the station announcements. So instead of finding out what would rhyme with 'Ian St John and Roger Hunt,' Nelson heard that his train was ready for boarding.

★

Searching in a stuffed kitchen drawer for matches, Abi also found an exercise book with '¡FUNDING PROPOSAL!' written on the cover. Within easy reach of the kettle and radio, the book helped Abi complete a mental image of what Max got up to out of bed most nights. Flicking past the first twenty pages of notes from meetings, telephone numbers, mission statements and calculations trying to match estimates of rent with targets for income, Abi found a series of poems slanting across the pages. The handwriting betrayed the half-light and drooping eyelids that accompanied the writing. The poems were often preceded by belligerent or bizarre quotes from politicians, soldiers or embedded Radio Four war reporters. There was some good stuff there, Abi noted, but it wouldn't necessarily play so well to a party crowd. The latest piece was entitled *Day 27* and simply read:

Fifteen thousand Iraqis are dead
My son is one

Abi tossed the book back in the drawer and went to light the candle on Nelson's cake. There'd been countless benefits to having a child before many of their friends had grown up properly, let alone settled down. Nelson was at ease with people of all ages and there was a whole community, for whom he was something of a mascot, looking out for him. As she reached for the light switch, though, Abi considered how much better it would have been to carry this cake into a room full of excited toddlers fresh from pass-the-parcel, rather than half-a-dozen adults, breaking off from the war chat to muster a *Happy Birthday* so grown-up and coherent, it could have been a New Seekers demo.

Judy and Will left shortly after the cake. They were on a rota to patrol the newsagents on Granby Street and Kingsley Road in case of arson attacks. Mickey had petrol bombs in mind as well.

'Just wanna blow something up now – know what I mean?' He rubbed his dark eyebrows with a marzipan-stained finger and thumb. 'This country, though – it's bringing out all my Irish nans and African ancestors, that's for sure – I ain't British, nor'anymore, like. Tell you another thing, they're not gerrin' me on that census, 'cos you *know* they're gonna use it when they bring the conscription back in. I'll be long gone, mate – cheap flight to Goa, *well* shot of this place... cheese!' Mickey added, as Nelson climbed onto the couch to plant the candle on his head, and Abi used up the last of the film in the camera.

Nelson had started to get the hang of photographs. He knew each one was going to become a memory, like that one of Will and Judy, Mum and Dad and everyone in their shiny clothes when he was a baby, which he remembered because he wasn't in it. When he blew out the candle before, there'd been another photograph. It would be a memory of something disappearing. It made sense to Nelson. Something, not just the candlelight and not just the cake, had ended. This much he knew, and he decided that this was the knowledge that would stay with him the longest.

★

There it went. Out of the train window, the seaside blue began to blanch and recede. Nelson tried to tell himself that there wasn't a different sky taking its place, that this was just the sort of bedtime story he used to tell himself and it had no meaning now. But he also knew he had to allow some kind of separation to take place. Tomorrow, he'd be flying out with the regiment for his first tour of duty. Whatever else he was going to do out there, he couldn't look up at the sky, nor at the moon at night, with its crescent turned up like a smile, and start thinking that this was the world he knew. Once he got off this train, he was going to stop remembering.

All Aboard the Liver Building

Paul Farley

It's not easy trying to explain how it all happened. A few years ago, I'd started having dreams about the Liver Building. Not nightmares exactly. I wasn't waking in a cold sweat. But my sleep would always be broken, and lying there, my heart racing at three or four o'clock, I'd find myself thinking of a clock face, glowing like a moon over a dark building, and slowly realise what it was.

I told my husband, but it wasn't an easy thing to talk about, not even in bed. Sometimes, I could hear him listening for a moment in the dark, but it was so bizarre, even by middle-of-the-night standards, that I'd usually hear his breathing change as he slipped back into his own dream. He could turn grumpy. What was I going on about now? Once, I got his attention by comparing the dream to a film.

'It's like in that Spielberg movie. About aliens.'

'*E.T*?'

'Before *E.T*. Where somebody can't stop thinking about that mountain.'

'What mountain?'

'He doodles it. He scoops it out of mashed potato at the dinner table. You know.'

I could hear his quiz brain tuning in. 'Oh. You mean *Close Encounters*. It's the Devil's Tower. In Wyoming. Or Montana. No, definitely Wyoming.' He paused, and then said, 'Ask me what the state capital of Wyoming is…'

He tried keeping a straight face when I'd ask him in broad daylight. 'It's the same as people who live in New

137

York. They never think about the Empire State Building, wouldn't dream of visiting it. Same with Parisians and the Eiffel Tower. Because it's just *there*. Since you've moved away from Liverpool, you've grown curious about it.' He thought on for a moment, and then said, 'Ask me how tall the Empire State Building is. In feet.'

The only thing to be done, the only way to get the Liver Building out of my head, was to go and visit it. I hadn't been to the Pier Head in years. Thinking on, I'd never actually been inside the Liver Building, or paid any attention to it when I lived in Liverpool. I wasn't sure whether I should make an appointment. What did they do in there? Something to do with insurance? I could pretend I needed to take out a new life policy.

In the event, it didn't matter. I told my husband I was visiting my mother, but spent a whole afternoon walking the streets that surround it. I even braved the ferry over to Birkenhead and back, just so I could frame the waterfront in its picture postcard view. But I preferred being closer.

This went on for months. Twice a week, and then three times a week, I'd take the train to Lime Street in the morning and spend the day around the Pier Head, looking at the Liver Building. I told my husband my mother was ill. The visits didn't stop the dreams. If anything, they made things worse, like scratching an itch. I was becoming inflamed. I remember the first time I touched one of its walls, first time I rode in its lifts, first time I counted its twelve chimes at noon. At the end of each day, I'd hate having to leave. Deep harmonics rang through me at night.

Things went from bad to worse. I started stopping over, staying in one of the new boutique hotels that were springing up near the waterfront in the old bonded warehouses and grain stores and eye hospitals, until I even found one with a view of the building, within earshot of its bells. One day, arriving home from a three-day binge of gazing on the pinioned Liver Birds and pressing my cheek against its cool granite walls, I sensed the atmosphere in the house had changed. Oddness and absence. My husband didn't arrive home until well after dark. This wasn't a quiz night. I could smell the drink on him.

'How was Liverpool?'

'Oh. You know. The usual.'

'And your mother? How is she doing?'

'No change, really.'

'Is that right? No change?' I realised then I'd walked into a hole.

You can guess the rest. He'd phoned my mother, who'd told him she hadn't had a day sick since we went decimal. And no, she hadn't seen me in months. Why *didn't* I visit more often? He demanded to know where I'd been. Where I'd been staying. Who with.

How could I honestly answer that?

It was easier just to go along with his worst fears. He'd found a credit card statement, full of debits to hotels with an L1 postcode. I was seeing another man. Yes. I was lovesick. I wasn't looking after myself anymore. Look at the state of me. But I couldn't come out and tell him. A male rival was something he could deal with, given time. But this country's first steel framed concrete building? Who could handle that?

Things fell apart quickly. I moved back in with my mother – who was glad to be finally seeing a bit more of me – and just a short bus ride from the Liver Building.

Bliss.

Days spent in its big shadow, or sheltering in one of its doorways.

Lost days, days measured out by its quarter chimes and the shadow of a Liver Bird creeping up the side of some other, duller edifice.

Bad poems, written on scraps of paper and posted through its huge letterboxes at dawn.

Even though you make this waterfront
Famous the world over,
I can't help thinking you were meant
To stand and grace another

So sail out with the vanished fleets
And cross the western seas,
Manhattan below Fourteenth Street
Has many vacancies

I began to realise that the poetry was me falling back on words, and signalled the end of that first phase when words aren't needed. I began listening more carefully to its bell chimes, especially on the hour. I could hear something, there, in the long ringing between each strike of the hammer.

The Liver Building was speaking to me.

It spoke in a strange accent. Not Scouse, which is what you would have thought. More like the merchant voice of its day. As the building told me, 'I am a great, awkward, sentimental creature unused to civilization, but I have strength and whether you laugh at me or not I shall get what I want.' It had learned the voices of the architects who had designed it, but could also mimic workmen whistling, or the gulls and starlings that had flown around its scaffolding. 'My voice is fixed in another age I fear' it confided in its low granitic whisper.

Of course, nobody else could hear it, but I worked out that standing at a special spot on Water Street, just up from the newspaper kiosk, seemed to focus its voice, like the way wind can suddenly funnel hard at certain city corners.

We had odd conversations. Things it had seen, all the endless crowds of people embarking from the landing stage, the big ships which came less and less until finally whole days could go by without sight of so much as a tug.

It knew a lot, but being a building it hadn't seen much

of the world. It knew the language of finance and insurance, risks and futures, balance sheets. It could talk in great detail about the view across the river, or about the streets surrounding it. One day, it told me all about the newspaper kiosk I stood by. 'Its first owner was a Mr Swank, or Swankie to customers. He kept a length of ship's rope hung smouldering from his counter, so they could light their cigarettes...' It could keep this up for hours. You'd want to scream.

It even bitched about the 'Other Two' or 'these so-called Graces' as it referred to its neighbours. It especially had it in for the Cunard Building.

To be honest, sometimes, it was a bit of a one-way conversation.

I've given up a lot to be here, I'd say. Out in all weather, a gale cutting in off the river. Look at me. Bin liners around my legs to keep out the cold. The police asking me to move along. Our first tiff. Me shouting into the wind.

This was bound to happen. Sometimes, after we rowed, it would fall silent, and for long awkward moments was a building again, mute and solid like all the others, pigeon-grey in the rainy light. It was sulky when it wanted to be. The Liver Birds stood with their backs turned to each other clutching their copper-green sprigs of foliage spitefully. I was depressed. When it was bad, in the silence following a quarrel, I even thought of climbing up one of its bell towers and jumping.

I knew it'd have to end. But I couldn't see how I could break things off. Until one day it told me itself. It told me to fetch a bottle of champagne.

Why? There wasn't anything to celebrate. It took me hours traipsing around before I was robbed blind for a bottle of something fizzy. As soon as I got back, walking downhill past the India Buildings, it started to chime six o'clock, and told me what it wanted me to do. I was to admit that it was over, and to throw the bottle against its east-facing wall. I was then to turn away and leave, and not to look back. I looked around: I'd been arrested a few times around here, and now I was about to make a public nuisance of myself again. I waited until there was a lull in the passing pedestrians – who usually did their best to pretend I was invisible anyway – then I took aim and threw the bottle as hard as I could.

It smashed into smithereens. Then, like I was told, I turned away and began walking quickly back uphill and away. And that was the last time I ever set eyes on the Liver Building.

But I know exactly what happened next. As I walked off towards Lime Street station, back towards my old life – if it'd have me back – didn't I feel a rumbling coming up through the ground, like a tube train passing underfoot? Wasn't that the sound of the Liver Building inching free of its mooring, pulling up its pipe work and foundations like tree roots, trailing them behind it like a scraggy tail as it started to slide down towards the river? It must have been quite a sight, a building launched into the water like the hulk of a liner sliding out of its shed into the waves. Wasn't there a huge splash? At first, it must have bobbed unsteadily, struggling to right itself before turning to face west. And then, at a slow, stately pace, it would have started to sail. On its upper floors, underwriters in open plan offices must have come out from under their desks to look out on a view utterly transformed: the city, smaller now and pulling further away, with a gap in its iconic riverfront like a missing tooth. By the time I was on the train travelling home, it would have cleared the bar light buoy, and moved out into open sea. By the time it was dark, people in caravan parks in Prestatyn and Llandudno and Anglesey could have watched two small pale moons gliding slowly along the horizon. Sometime the next day it would have made open ocean, the big swell lifting and dropping its thousands of tonnes of concrete and steel and granite like seaweed, the bow waves crashing as high as its fourth floor. Barnacles couldn't believe their luck. At some point out in the mid-Atlantic, its *lifts* became *elevators*, and the numbers of its floors all shuffled down one. On and on it sails westward, making good speed, further and further out of mind and into the improbable, smaller and smaller, until my sleep is unbroken, and dreamless.

Contributors

Dinesh Allirajah is a founder of the North West writing group 'Asian Voices, Asian Lives'. He has performed at venues all over Europe and his short story collection *A Manner of Speaking* was publisahed by Spike Books in 2004.

Tracy Aston's work includes six plays for BBC Radio 4, and numerous scripts for the Unity Theatre, Liverpool, including two Christmas shows. For the past 11 years, she has been involved in many community writing, playmaking and reminiscence projects, for people with mental health problems, survivors of abuse, elders, children with disabilities, residents of HMP Liverpool and aspiring writers of all ages. She would like to acknowledge the elders in Halewood who contributed their stories to the Childhood and Working Lives Project which provided the inspiration for her story.

Beryl Bainbridge has been shortlisted for the Booker Prize five times. Her early novels draw on experiences of growing up in Liverpool, where she was expelled from school at the age of 14 and began acting on stage at the age of 16. Her experiences in the theatre formed the basis of *An Awfully Big Adventure* (1989), later made into a movie starring Hugh Grant. Since the 1990s she has written several historical novels, including: *The Birthday Boys* (1991), about the ill-fated expedition of Robert Falcon Scott; *Every Man for Himself* (1996), about the wreck of the Titanic; *Master Georgie* (1998) about the Crimean War; and *According to Queeney*

(2001), about Samuel Johnson. Her other novels include *Another Part of the Wood* (1968), *Young Adolf* (1978) and *Winter Garden* (1980).

Clive Barker is one of the world's leading authors and directors of contemporary horror/fantasy, writing prolifically in the late 70s and throughout the 80s, mostly in the form of short stories (collected in *Books of Blood 1–6*), as well as the Faustian novel *The Damnation Game* (1986). Later he moved toward modern-day fantasy and urban fantasy with horror elements in *Weaveworld* (1987), *The Great and Secret Show* (1989), the world-spanning *Imajica* (1991) and *Sacrament* (1996). His film work includes 1987's *Hellraiser*, which he directed and adapted from his novella *The Hellbound Heart*. The story in this anthology was the inspiration for the 1992 blockbuster *Candyman*, and its two sequels.

Ramsey Campbell is described by the Oxford Companion to English Literature as 'Britain's most respected living horror writer' and in 1991 was voted the Horror Writer's Horror Writer in the *Observer Magazine*. He sold his first story, 'The Church in the High Street', to August Derleth in 1962. Leaving school that same year, his first collection, *The Inhabitant of the Lake and Less Welcome Tenants* appeared from Derleth's Arkham House imprint two years later. Although his early fiction was heavily influenced by H.P. Lovecraft's *Cthulhu Mythos* (yet set in a distinctly British milieu), his subsequent books and stories have revealed him to be a unique voice in horror fiction. His many award-winning novels include *The Face That Must Die, Incarnate,* and most recently *The Overnight* (PS Publishing).

Frank Cottrell Boyce is a novelist and screenwriter. His film credits include *Welcome to Sarajevo, Hilary and Jackie, 24 Hour Party People* and *A Cock and Bull Story*. In 2004, his debut novel *Millions* won the Carnegie Medal and was shortlisted for The Guardian Children's Fiction Award. His second novel, *Framed,* was published by Macmillan in 2005.

Paul Farley studied at the Chelsea School of Art and has lived in London, Brighton, Cumbria and Lancashire. His work has been widely anthologised in collections such as *New British Poetry, Being Alive, Poems on the Underground, 52 Ways of Looking at a Poem* and *Poem for the Day.* He has had two collections published by Picador, *The Boy from the Chemist is Here to See You*, and *The Ice Age.* A new poetry collection, *Tramp in Flames,* and a BFI Modern Classic, *Distant Voices, Still Lives*, are published this year.

James Friel's most recent novel is *The Higher Realm.* His next, *A Posthumous Affair,* will be published in the US in 2009, as well as a collection of short stories, *The Age of Reason.* He is Programme Leader for the MA in Writing at the Centre for Writing, Liverpool John Moores University.

Margaret Murphy is the author of eight critically acclaimed psychological crime novels. Her first, *Goodnight My Angel,* was shortlisted for the First Blood award for debut crime fiction. She is a member of the Society of Authors and the Crime Writers' Association, and a founder member of Murder Squad, a touring collective of crime writers. Winner of the year 2000 CWA Leo Harris Award, she reviews crime fiction and regularly writes articles for *Crime Time*, as well as being a contributor to Radio 4's *The Message.*

Brian Patten made his name in the 60s as one of three breakthrough Liverpool poets, with Adrian Henri and Roger McGough, through the publication of the ground-breaking anthology, *The Mersey Sound* (1967). His own collections include *Little Johnny's Confession* (1967), *Vanishing Trick* (1976), *Love Poems* (1981), *Storm Damage* (1988), and *Armada* (1996). He is a popular broadcaster and editor, and is author of several best-selling poetry collections for children, most famously *Gargling with Jelly: A Collection of Poems* (1985) and *Juggling with Gerbils* (2000). This is his first short story.

Eleanor Rees was born in Birkenhead in 1978. Her first poetry pamphlet, *Feeding Fire* (Spout) received an Eric Gregory Award in 2002. Her first full collection, *Andraste's Hair* (Salt, 2007) was shortlisted for the Forward First Collection Prize. She lives in Liverpool and works as a poet in the community.

Special Thanks

The publisher would like to thank the following people for their support, expertise and patience in the delivery of this project: Mike Morris, Madeline Henaghan, Bryan Biggs, Maura Kennedy, Ailsa Cox, Robert Shephard, Alicia Stubbersfield, Jenny Newman, Adrian Mealing, Dave Ward, Cara Jones, Edward Wilson, Eileen Godlis, Jenny Hewson, Carrie Rooney, Charlotte Riches, Justine Potter and Duncan Minshull. Comma would particularly like to thank Isaac Shaffer, who edited *Leeds Stories 1 & 2*, and Tane Page who edited *Liverpool Stories 1* – two pamphlet projects on which this Book of the City series is based. Without their efforts, this anthology and its sister title, *The Book of Leeds,* would never have come about.

ALSO AVAILABLE IN THE SERIES...

The Book of Leeds
A CITY IN SHORT FICTION

Edited by Maria Crossan & Tom Palmer

ISBN 1-905583-01-X
EAN 978-1-905583-01-0
RRP: £7.95

Featuring:

Tony Harrison
Jeremy Dyson
Shamshad Khan
Ian Duhig
David Peace
Susan Everett
M.Y. Alam
Andrea Semple
Martyn Bedford
& Tom Palmer

The Book of Leeds is anthology of ten short stories set in and around the city's streets. The book reflects the quality and breadth of writing by contemporary Leeds authors, including acclaimed poets, novelists, short story writers, and screenwriters – all brought together in a fictional exploration of the city.

The book features stories set in each decade of the last 50 years, stories that detail how Leeds has evolved from a post-war city falling into decline after the demise of the textile trade, through to its emergence as a successful modern city, with both problems and promise.